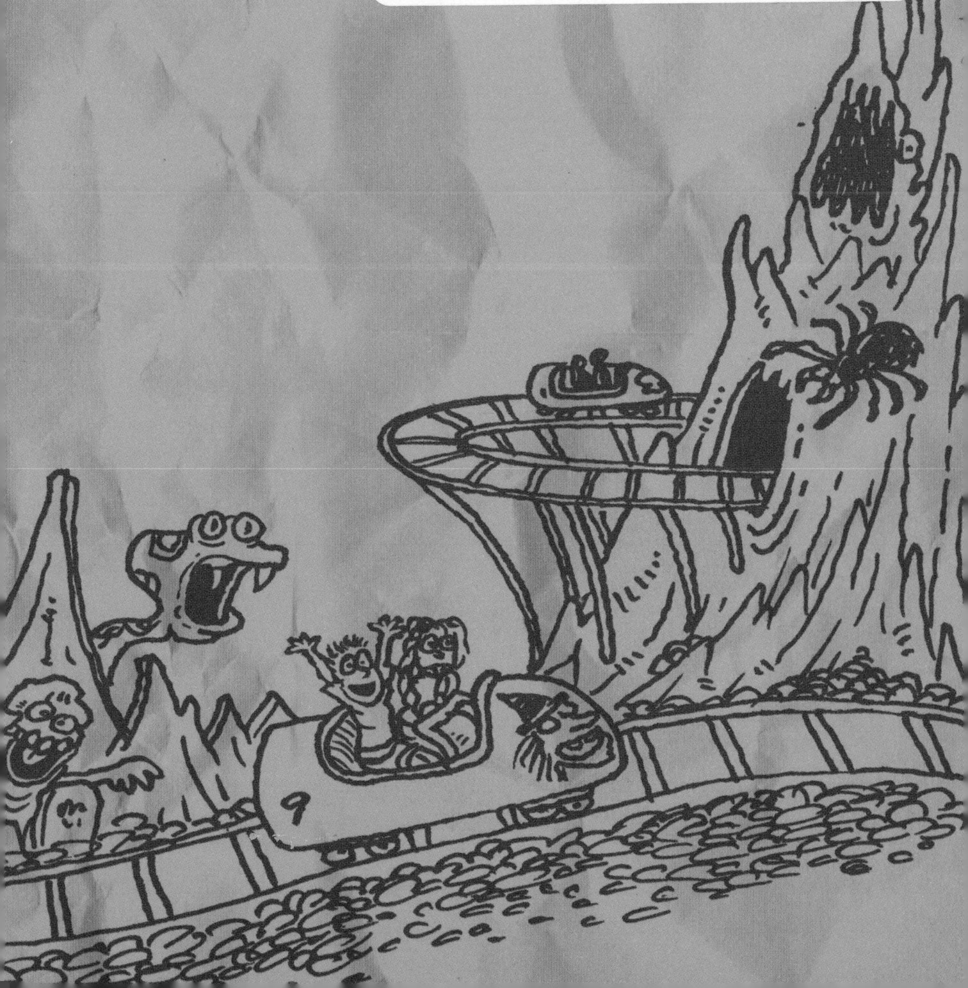

DESMOND PUCKET

AND the
MOUNTAIN FULL OF MONSTERS

Other books by Mark Tatulli

DESMOND PUCKET

and the

MOUNTAIN FULL OF MONSTERS

Andrews McMeel
Publishing

Kansas City • Sydney • London

1 THE FOG OF DESMOND

Something's wrong.

You know that kind of wrong, like when you put your underpants on backwards by mistake: everything looks like it's supposed to, but something just doesn't feel right.

I sit up, reach over to my bedside table, and grab my official limited-edition Ray Harryhausen *Jason and the Argonauts* saber-skeleton talking alarm clock.

". . . and how can it be light outside if it's the middle of the night!"

Then I notice the skeleton isn't making his usual chattering teeth sound. And he's not crazily swinging his sabers in his typical skeletonly way. In fact, it's like he's dead.

OK, right, a dead skeleton is a normal skeleton. But in this case it's making me nervous.

I spring out of bed and bolt over to my bulletin board. I begin tearing through the billion-and-two scraps of paper and ideas that are tacked to every bit of empty cork board space.

Mom bought me this bulletin board so I would stop leaving little ideas and cartoons all over my desk. Now I just pin them all over my wall.

Eventually I find the old brochure that I'm looking for . . .

. . . but most important, the Post-it note that's stuck to the bottom.

"Today is May twenty-fifth," I say out loud. "But what time is it?!"

I dig through the mounds of plastic fangs, rubber spiders, and tubes of fake blood in my top desk drawer and find my official 60th anniversary *Creature from the Black Lagoon* commemorative wristwatch. I pop open the cover.

"Hot dog! I still have five minutes!"

I get dressed with lightning speed, fly down the stairs without touching a single step, and spring out the front door! The walk to Cloverfield Memorial Junior High is usually long, but today I run it in record time. And I know I'm safe when I see my class waiting at the curb for the bus. I race up to Ricky DiMarco, trying to catch my breath.

Yes, that's right . . . no pants. All alone in my tighty whities. In front of the entire sixth grade class.

Sheila Cutter screams and slips into a witch-like cackle. Scott Seltzer laughs so hard that an entire Sour Patch Kid candy flies out of his nose. And everybody, yes, everybody, pulls out their cell phones . . .

. . . and starts making the viral video of the century. Even Tina Schimsky, the love of my life and dream girl extraordinaire, who adds her own blow-by-blow commentary.

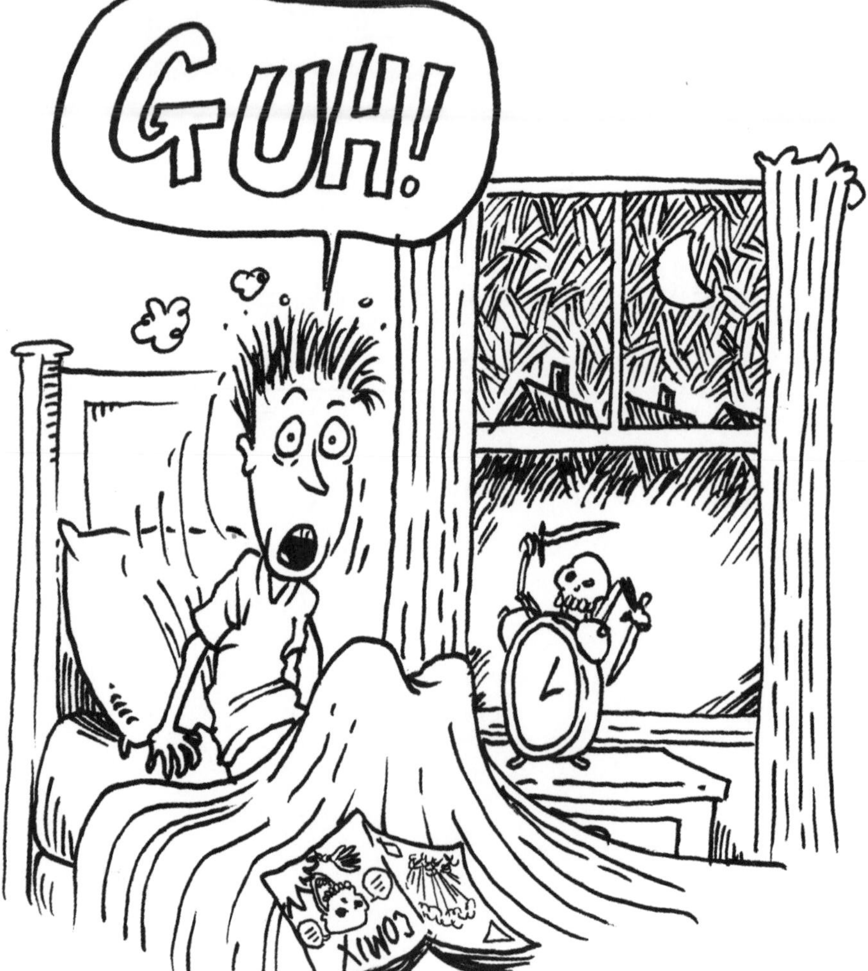
GUH!
COMIX

2 GO TIME

A stupid dream.

My *Jason and the Argonauts* skeleton clock is still clattering away, just like always. The alarm will go off on time. I won't run out of the house in just my underpants. And I won't miss the sixth grade trip to Crab Shell Pier. Or the Mountain Full of Monsters ride, which basically I've been waiting for my whole life.

"I know! This is a good chance to go over the plan!"

I walk across my bed, jump into my thinking chair, and pop on my desk lamp. And, of course, I pull out my giant spiral notebook of scary effects and gross ideas . . .

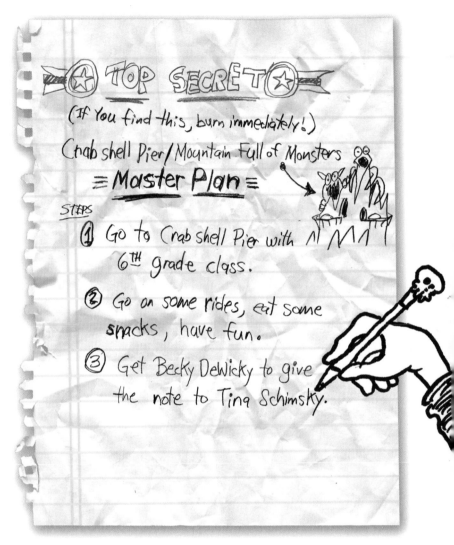

I look at step 3. The note. The note that I carefully wrote the day I found out I was allowed to go on the sixth grade trip to Crab Shell Pier. I carried it in my wallet for weeks. I better check it again.

I pull the bit of folded paper out of my vintage *Fiend Without a Face* collectors' billfold.

Yeah. That seems right to the point. Maybe I should add a "please" here and there? Nah, I don't want to sound too whiney and begging.

Truth is, ever since the success of my epic monster magic show last month (that used to be Mr. Bramfield's boring musical), things sort of changed for me. And suddenly just going on the Mountain Full of Monsters ride by myself isn't enough anymore . . .

But before I drift off into this thought, I set my miniature replica Lon Chaney *Phantom of the Opera* alarm clock to 7 a.m. *and* super-organ blast . . . just to be sure. Because when it's about to be the best day of your whole life, you really don't want to sleep through it!

3 A FUNNY THING HAPPENED ON THE WAY TO THE BUS STOP

I guess I should have warned you.

Ricky lives with his grandparents, and they're really into Christmas. Really, really into Christmas. Like even now, when it's May.

"Uh, Merry Christmas, Mr. and Mrs. DiMarco. Is Ricky ready?"

"Oh, Desmond, you bad boy," Ricky's grandmother says, grabbing my hand and pretend-slapping the top of it. "Remember, we're Mr. and Mrs. Mistletoe!"

"Would you like some hot cocoa and a candy cane while you wait for Ricky?"

"Oh, no, thank you, Mrs. DiM—Mrs. Mistletoe. We have to catch a bus."

"Right, yes, the class trip! Let me hustle up Ricky then. You go wait in the Rudolph room."

Not only are Ricky's grandparents totally into Christmas, but they even divided their house into "theme rooms." The Rudolph room is all reindeer, the Santa room is full of every kind of Santa Claus decoration, and on like that. But my favorite is the North Pole room!

It's like another world! And the coolest thing is the snow machine that pumps fake flakes 24/7!

Ricky's grandparents used to dress up as Santa and Mrs. Claus and drive around the country in this giant caravan called the *Santa Express*.

The DiMarcos in the jingle days!

Merry Christmas!

But then they had to stop to take care of Ricky, so they parked the old beast out back next to the shed . . .

Santa Express!

. . . and it hasn't moved since.

For as long as I can remember, Ricky has lived with his grandparents in this non-stop Christmas fantasy. Everybody thinks the DiMarcos are nuts and Ricky catches a lot of guff about them at school. But I think this whole Christmas trip is amazing and I couldn't even imagine growing up with so much awesome!

"Now, Ricky, where's your jacket?" says Mrs. DiMarco, following us to the door. "It's going to get cold later and—"

"It's in my backpack, Gram. I'll be fine!"

"Have fun today, you two! And if you see any nifty Christmas decorations at Crab Shell Pier, pick them up for me and I'll give you the money later!"

"OK, we've got fifteen minutes until we get to school," I say, changing the subject. "We should go over the plan."

Ricky smiles and I can tell he's thinking about Becky DeWicky. Ricky's not totally into Becky or anything, but she's a girl he knows, and the big picture of our plan is to get on the Mountain Full of Monsters ride with both Becky and Tina Schimsky. But you can't just jump right into these things. You need a plan.

But there's one thing that definitely *isn't* part of the plan . . .

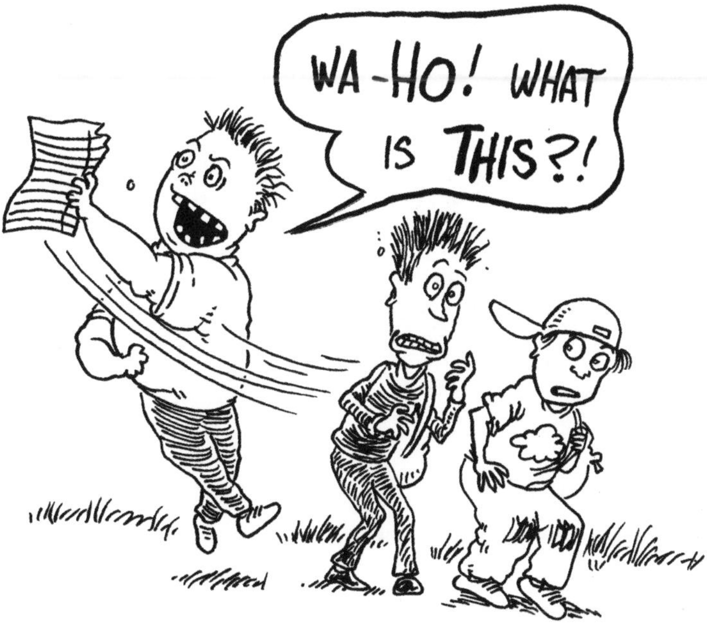
WA-HO! WHAT IS THIS?!

. . . Scott Seltzer!

4 SCOTT SELTZER: ANATOMY OF A DILLWEED

Scott Seltzer isn't the punch-you-in-the-chest, old school kind of bully. He's just a first-class jerk.

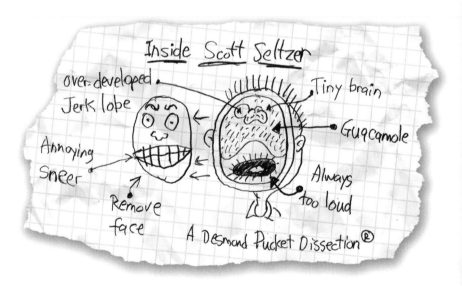

Inside Scott Seltzer

over-developed Jerk lobe

Annoying Sneer

Remove face

Tiny brain

Guacamole

Always too loud

A Desmond Pucket Dissection®

He's a fart at a funeral. The snow that doesn't stick. The rug fuzz in the Play-Doh.

Scott's always there when you don't want him, and never there when you really need him.

But the really funny thing about Scott is, we used to be friends!

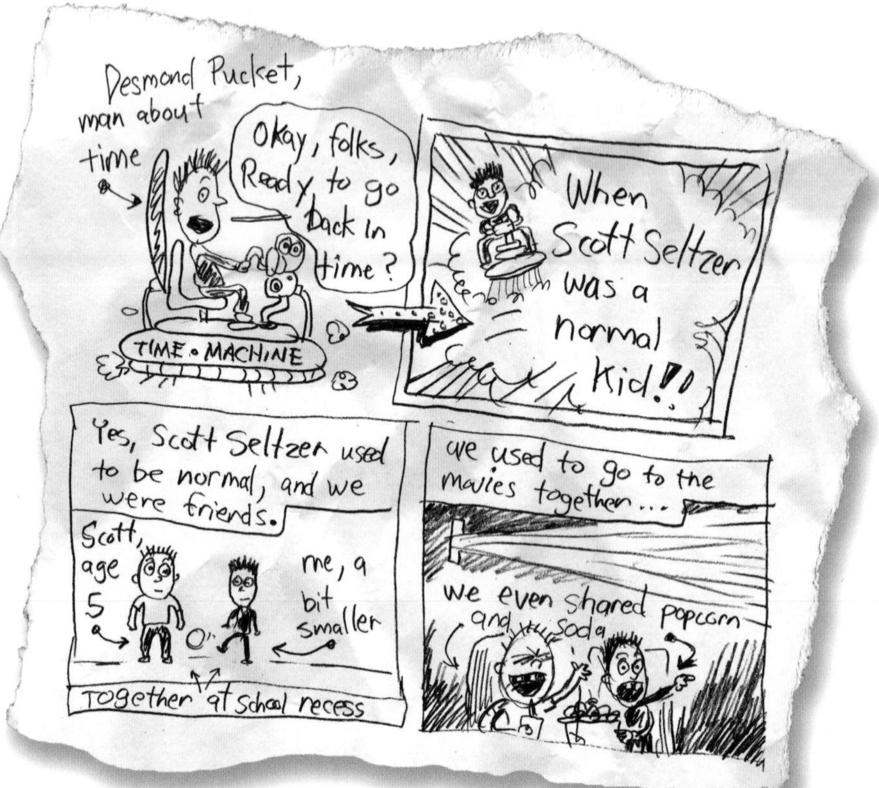
Desmond Pucket, man about time
Okay, folks, Ready, to go back in time?
TIME • MACHINE
When Scott Seltzer was a normal kid!!
Yes, Scott Seltzer used to be normal, and we were friends.
Scott, age 5
me, a bit smaller
Together at school recess
we used to go to the movies together...
we even shared popcorn
and soda

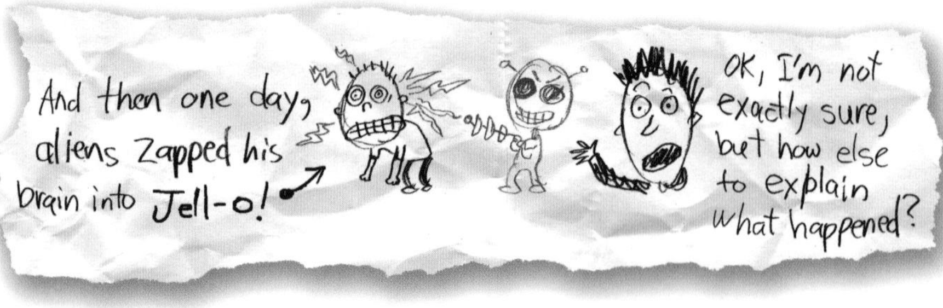
And then one day, aliens zapped his brain into Jell-o!
OK, I'm not exactly sure, but how else to explain what happened?

My birthday was coming up, and of course Scott was invited to the party. Little did he know, it would be a *surprise* party!

The day came and my house was packed with kids. And as usual, Scott was right in the front.

And from that day forward, we were no longer feuding friends, but mortal enemies!

And, just like old times, Scott is grabbing something that's mine . . . the super-secret plans!

Suddenly a hand comes out of nowhere . . .

. . . and yanks the paper out of Scott's hand.

It's always a shock to me that Tina Schimsky actually knows my name!

Little does Tina know, she just rescued the plan to our almost-soon-to-be Mountain Full of Monsters first date!

5 FINALLY THERE

I stare hard out of the bus window. Can it really be true? I rub my eyes and look again.

It doesn't go away. We're really here! Crab Shell Pier! And somewhere in that tangle of rides is the Mountain Full of Monsters!

Ricky and I jump out of our seats and join in the crush of kids squeezing out of the small bus door. Suddenly I feel a jerk on my backpack, and I'm pulled to the back of the line. I spin around, "Scott, you are in big trouble now . . ."

Crud! It's Mr. Needles, head of our school's disciplinary office! I forgot: he's one of the chaperones on this class trip! And he's personally been assigned to me! I look for an escape route, but it's like Needles reads my mind; he grabs the handle of my backback, holding me like a suitcase.

"And look," he says, pulling a piece of folded notebook paper out of his fanny pack. "I have a whole plan of educational activities that we can partake in at Crab Shell Pier! Things I'm sure you didn't even know existed!"

Oh, no! Mr. Needles has a plan, too! And it's totally going to ruin *my* plan! What am I going to do?!

I look at Ricky and point to the men's room door by the entrance to the pier. Ricky nods.

"Mr. Needles, we have to go to the bathroom."

He looks at us suspiciously. And then he releases his grip on my backpack.

"Don't take too long," he snarls.

Ricky and I bang through the door of the restroom and immediately attack the situation.

"No way, Ricky! Crab Shell Pier isn't that big; Needles will track us down! That's what he wants us to do!"

"Make him run from us?" Ricky says. "How we gonna do that?"

I pull out my brochure of Crab Shell Pier. Inside is a map of all the rides and attractions in the place.

" . . . I think our answer is right here!"

6 DITCHING NEEDLES

"I was getting worried about you boys," quips Mr. Needles. "I was about to send in a search party!"

"So, fellas, what's it going to be first?" Mr. Needles asks. "Since we're going to be together all day, I thought we'd start out with something fun!"

"Well said, Mr. Pucket!" Mr. Needles replies. "Perhaps you are ready to put away childish things like monsters and mayhem!"

The Technology Shack is one of those boring amusement attractions that mixes fun with learning.

Or pretends to anyway. We all know it's just there to make parents feel better about bringing their kids to a fun place like Crab Shell Pier, which has no educational value and will probably end up making them puke and get cavities.

"OK, dude," I whisper to Ricky. "You entertain Mr. Needles while I take care of business!"

Great! Needles is distracted! But I'm not going to have much time! I sure hope this works!

"Hey, Richard!" Mr. Needles says excitedly, "Did you know that the original form of home video was called Betamax and actually was superior in record/playback quality to VHS?"

Bzzzzzzzzzzz! Bzzzzzzzzzzz! Bzzzzzzzzzzz!

"Listen, fellas, I'd love to continue this educational journey with you, but my services are required back at the fort! Just check in with one of the other chaperones . . ."

And just like that . . .

. . . Mr. Needles is off like a shot.

"I grabbed up one of those old phones from the '90s . . . they're easy as pie to program and make a text message look like it's coming from anybody!"

"Ah," says Ricky. "Even the school principal! Man oh man, Needles is gonna be mad as a hatter when he finds out. Principal Badonkus, too!"

"You're right, Ricky. So we better get in as much of Crab Shell Pier as possible, while we still can."

7 OUT AND ABOUT ON CRAB SHELL PIER

OK, Mr. Needles is out of the picture (for now), so let's get back to the plan. I pull the list out.

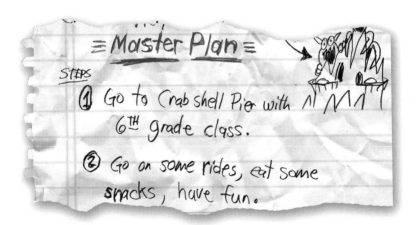

Step one, **check!**

Step two, the next order of business! Time to explore the wildness that is known as Crab Shell Pier.

Crab Shell Pier was built way back in the 1950s, and they've never torn down anything since; they just keep layering the new stuff over the old. So it just grows and grows, like some kid's giant Lego set. Only they keep adding parts that don't match the Legos, like Tinker Toys and Lincoln Logs and K'NEX and lots of wires, rubber bands, and electric tape.

Now the whole thing is one humongous, awesome, twisted mess of metal rides, wooden coasters, squirting and spinning and shooting games, candy, popcorn, and fudge shops, cheeseburger-on-a-stick and deep-fried saltwater taffy stands. In other words, kid heaven. But the one thing that has always stayed the same is the Mountain Full of Monsters ride!

Ricky and I worm our way through the mass of kids pressed all around the ticket booths, the huge lines for the rides snaking everywhere. Man, every sixth grade class in the country must be here today! Ricky jumps in line to get tickets for the thrill rides, but right now my brain is only in one place: even though we're saving it for last, I just have to see The Mountain Full of Monsters before I do another thing!

My mind is focused on this one thought, which is probably why I don't see the fist coming.

I'd know those knuckles anywhere . . . the patented Becky DeWicky "Hello."

Becky was the brains behind the electronics of my epic Monster Magic show. If it hadn't been for her, I never would have been able to pull it off. But that doesn't make my arm hurt any less.

"Oh, right! The Mountain Full of Monsters," she says. "Are you going on that now?"

"No, we're going on it last because—" and then I stop and remember the plan: **Step three** . . .

③ Get Becky DeWicky to give the note to Tina Schimsky.

OK, maybe I'm jumping the gun a bit, but I get excited and the time seems right.

"Hey, Becky, you know Tina Schimsky, right?" I say as I pull the note out of my wallet. "Can you give this to her?"

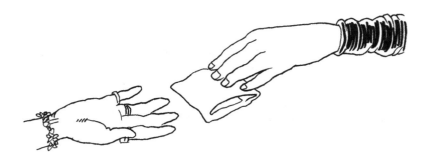

"Well, I'm not giving it to her unless I can read it first," she replies, unfolding the crumpled paper.

"No, that's priv—!" I reach out, but I'm too slow.

From the Desk of
DESMOND PUCKET
"Gourmet of Gore"

Hi, Tina, it's Desmond Pucket.
I'm the kid who made a
horror show out of the school play.
Would you go on the "Mountain
Full of Monsters" ride with me?

YES ☐   NO ☐

(check one and return to
Becky DeWicky)

"Are you kidding with this?!" Becky yells, and then throws the note in my face.

OK, wait . . . so what just happened now?

Becky is my pal. My bud. Always been.

Why doesn't she want to help? Isn't that what friends are for?

So it looks like my plan is falling apart. Time to start thinking about a Plan B. I bend down to get my note . . .

. . . but I'm just a second too late!

Uh, hello! Isn't this supposed to be the best day of my whole life?!

What's happening?!

8 THE CRAZY CHASE

Scott Seltzer runs off and melts into the ocean of kids surrounding the Swiss Bob ride.

Luckily, I can see his chubby fingers holding my note above the heads of the crowd. He's moving slower because of the mass of people, and I close the space between us.

I can't believe it! Just as I'm about to grab my note, Scott hands it off to Grub Wasserstein, one of his minions who's strapped into the ride! Suddenly the brakes of the Swiss Bob shriek and the fake bobsleds lurch forward, taking Grub Wasserstein and my note for Tina with them!

But as the ride picks up speed and Grub Wasserstein flings his arms up, I realize what's going to
happen.

My note escapes into the wind and I race along
after it.

And once again, it falls into the hands of the enemy. This time it's StinkEye Blanchard, . . .

. . . another of Scott's agents of evil. Proudly waving the note, StinkEye bolts into the Wacky Shack funhouse. I chase after her.

I dash up the stairs and burst through the funhouse door into inky blackness.

I can hear StinkEye's jittery laugh echoing ahead of me in the dark and I head toward the noise. As I creep forward, I see a shaft of light. Another room.

A maze of mirrors and glass walls!

I can see StinkEye running through the maze with my note, but she's always on the other side of the glass or just a reflection. Suddenly she smooshes her face into the glass wall right in front of me.

Normally I'm a fan of gross-ocity, but the snot and skin smears StinkEye leaves behind are not something I ever want to see twice in my lifetime!

I make my way through the mirrored halls until I find myself in the funhouse tunnel. I spot StinkEye, just ahead of me!

The problem is the tunnel is spinning and it's really hard to move in something that's churning you around like cement in a mixer. StinkEye is definitely better at it. Probably because she has suckers on her hands like an octopus. That's my theory, anyway.

And just as we're about to make the trade, the tunnel spins in the opposite direction, . . .

. . . knocking us both on our butts and sending the loose sneaker and note flying around us.

I'm inches away from grabbing the runaway paper and ending this crazy chase when suddenly . . .

. . . the note flies out of the mouth
of the tunnel, floats down into the crowd below,

. . . and lands . . .

. . . right at the feet of Tina Schimsky!

9 YOUR ATTENTION, PLEASE

Tina Schimsky sees the note! She's going to pick up my note!

The cutest girl in the entire sixth grade at Cloverfield Memorial Junior High School is going to read the note that I wrote to her! My plan just might work out after all!

Once again, Scott Seltzer appears at the worst possible moment! What a talent he has for that! Before Tina can even react, Scott lunges over to the Inflate-A-Baboon game and grabs the barker's microphone.

"I shall now read from the note of Desmond Pucket, addressed to Tina Schimsky," Scott's greasy voice booms out from the giant gray loudspeaker mounted over the game area. The crowd begins to quiet as I watch in helpless horror from the balcony of the Wacky Shack.

Meanwhile, a pier security guy and a handful of the chaperones try to stop Scott, but he scampers up and out of reach. They have no idea the level of advanced dill-weediness they are dealing with.

"Love always and forever, Desmond Pucket!" Scott finishes with a flourish in his best stage actor's voice.

OK, Scott changed my words to the most embarrassing ones he could think of, but he did get the spirit of the note right. Still, I couldn't help noticing that Tina cringed during the whole thing.

The crowd turns into one giant laughing mob and Scott bows as he slides down to the ground and into the hands of the angry chaperones.

The laughter grows louder and I start to formulate Plan C: *My Escape from Crab Shell Pier*.

"Your attention, please," a different voice suddenly crackles out of the speakers, cutting through the howls of laughter. *"Your attention, please!"*

The crowd hushes.

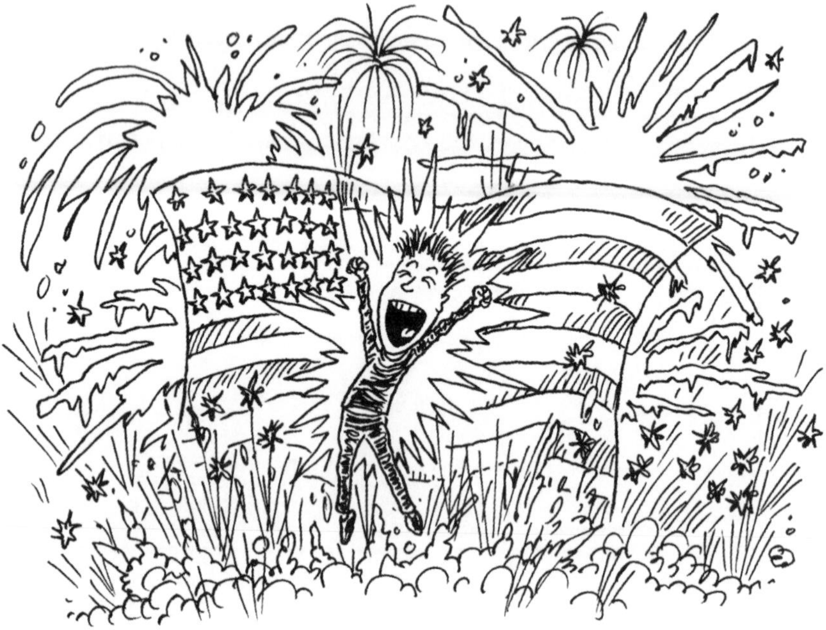

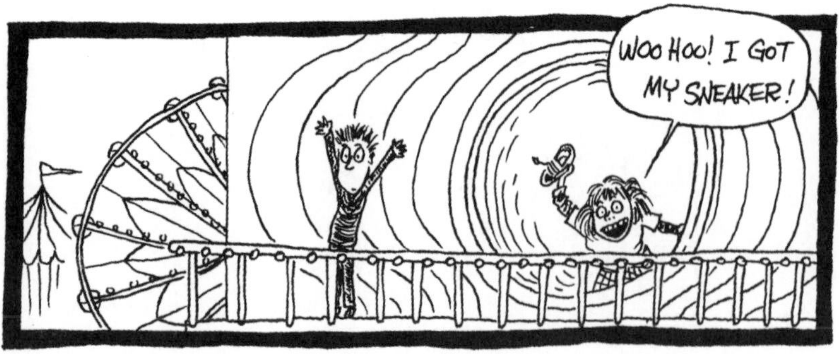
WOO HOO! I GOT MY SNEAKER!

10 MOUNTAIN FULL OF MONSTERS, PART ONE

Too good to be true! Tina Schimsky and me! Together! On the Mountain Full of Monsters ride! Is this really happening?

I decide to ignore the beasties.

Stomach failure is not an option when you're standing next to the girl of your dreams and about to go on the greatest amusement ride in the world.

And there it is . . .

For a second, I just stand there and gasp at all this amazing monsterly awesomeness, this gargantuan beast of a spook-house mountain, crawling with moving animatronic creatures, ghosts, skulls, claws, and tentacles! A huge animated dragon, whose giant snake-like body coils around the entire mountain, sporadically spews fire and smoke with a loud . . .

. . . momentarily hushing the excited crowd waiting on line.

The coolest thing is, the Mountain Full of Monsters used to be just an old rollercoaster called the Wild Mouse.

"Wild Mouse" Roller Coaster. →

AAAAA! AAAAAA!

← Single cars go around a Swirly track.

The pier folks built fake rocks and caves around it; they made a mountain out of a mouse hill as the saying sort of goes.

Then they filled the mountain with every kind of animated bugaboo, bogie man, goblin, and ghoul they could find from old out-of-business haunted house rides. A recycled horror show, I guess you could say. And I totally mean that with respect!

Good point.

Luckily, Ricky appears before I can say anything else stupid.

"Hey, dudes," he says, smiling his goofy Ricky smile that he saves for awkward situations, like whenever he's around girls, "I got four tickets. We should get in line."

The other ticket, of course, is for Becky DeWicky, who is giving me a look like I just ate her last tater tot.

I look over at Ricky who is using his Whoopee cushion to clear a path through the long line of kids.

"Well, he *is* going to get us onto the ride faster, that's for sure."

I walk forward and stand next to Tina. As we get closer to the front of the line, I can see she is getting nervous. The rickety cars roar around the tracks, in and out of caves, and screams echo over the creepy organ music. Now Tina's biting her fingers. Should I reach for her hand? Would that be too weird? What should I do?

Suddenly my brain jumps back in time . . . girl advice from the old man:

Holy crud, *that* was useless! It's a wonder Dad ever married anyone! I squeeze my eyes tight to try and shake away the memory when suddenly . . .

. . . the dragon lets loose a humongous fireball and

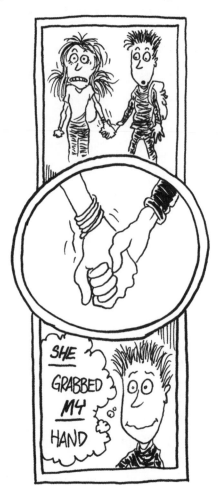

SHE GRABBED MY HAND

Well, what do you know? Who would've thought the best move would be . . . nothing at all.

When Ricky sees me and Tina holding hands, he decides to make his move. And Becky makes hers.

Poor Ricky! I'm going to have to give him some pointers.

Finally, we get to the front of the line and it's our turn to board the Mountain Full of Monsters. It's all happening just as I dreamed! As the little car pulls in front of us I try to memorize everything about it . . .

. . . because I want to remember every detail of the greatest day of my life, for the rest of my life!

I jump in the car, fasten my safety harness, and when I turn to help Tina—

This ride is about to be scarier than I thought.

11 MOUNTAIN FULL OF MONSTERS, PART TWO

"Yes, Mr. Pucket, it didn't take me long to figure out your little text message from Principal Badonkus was a fake," Mr. Needles says triumphantly from the seat that Tina Schimsky is supposed to be sitting in.

I don't believe it! Mr. Needles bumped Tina out of the line and cut in! And now he's about to pull me off the Mountain Full of Monsters ride and ruin everything!

But just as Mr. Needles is yanking me out, his foot gets tangled in the safety strap. Even as he tugs and pulls, our little pretzel car lurches forward to begin its journey into the dark mountain.

"You can't, sir, the ride is already in motion," yells the operator. "You have to sit! You are endangering the other passengers and violating park rules!"

Realizing that our car is now almost at the cave entrance, Mr. Needles obediently drops into his seat and pulls the strap tight.

"I don't want to break the rules," Mr. Needles says to me, nervously. "You're already in enough trouble as it is!"

I peek over and suddenly it dawns on me . . .

I turn around for one last look at the gang.

Well . . . this not exactly going as I had planned, but at least I'm finally experiencing the Mountain Full of Monsters! And it's going to be awesome, even with Mr. Needles next to me making little nervous baby sniffly noises.

The car approaches the skull entrance and *bang!*

We punch through the doors and into the pitch dark!

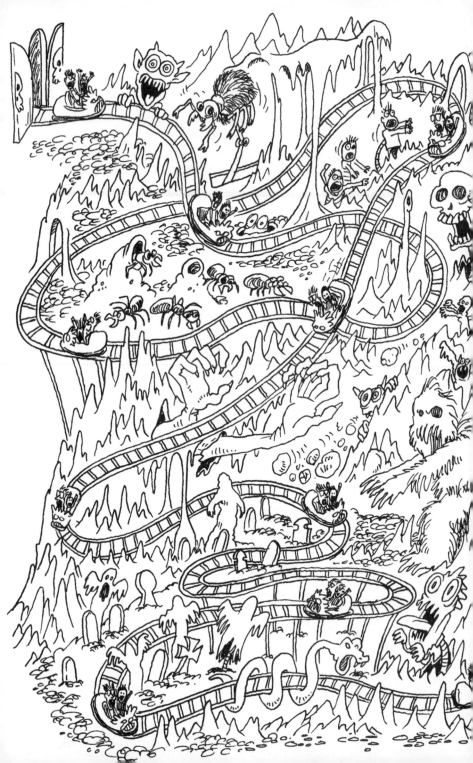

Follow along and see if Mr. Needles
can keep from blowing chunks!!!

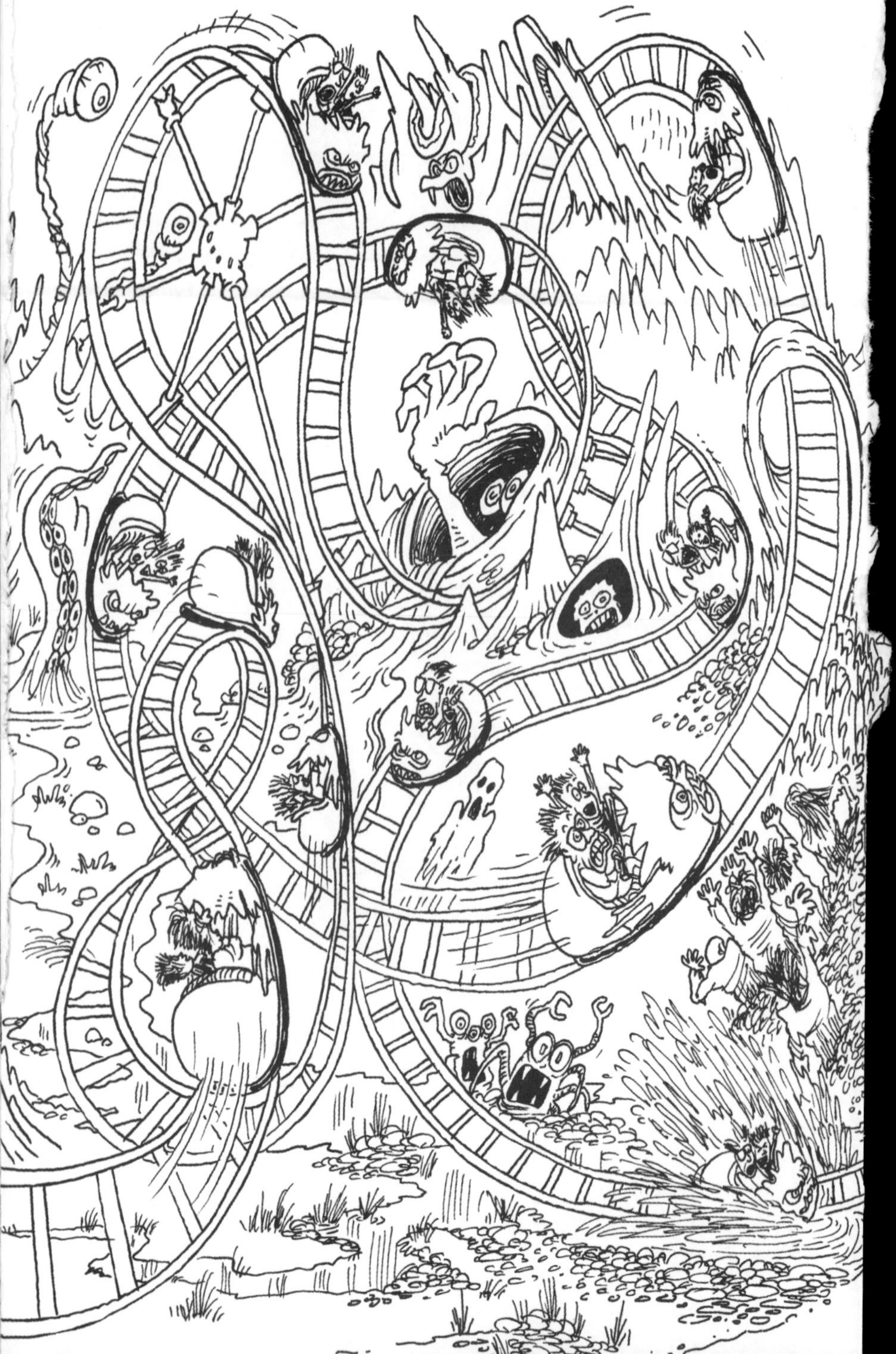

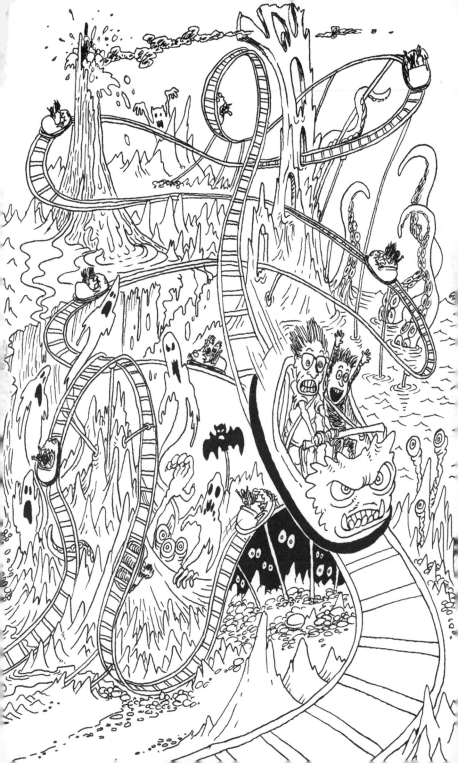

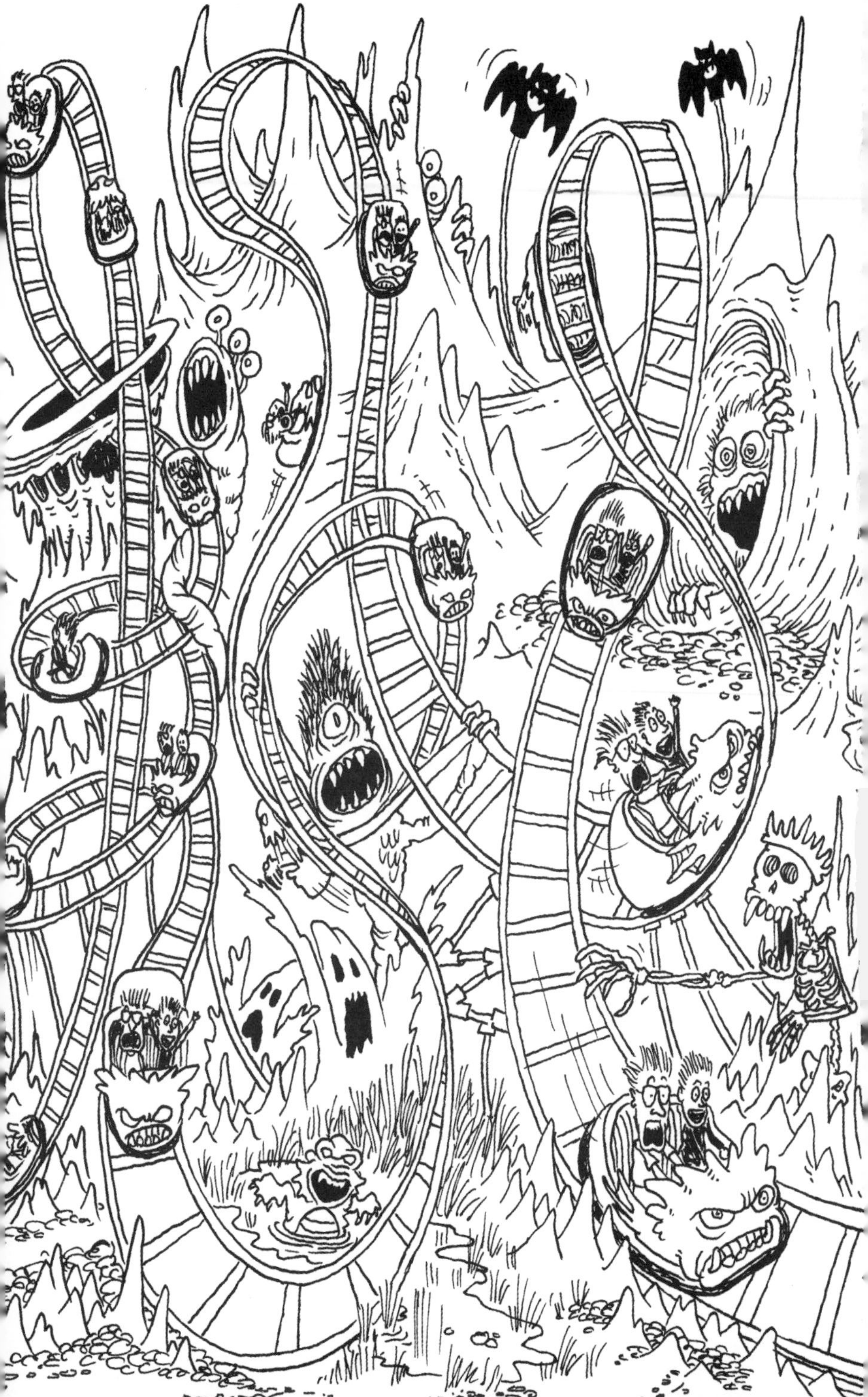

Our little car suddenly bursts through the exit doors and the ride's brakes squeal, jerking us to an abrupt stop. The car eases forward to let us out, pick up the new passengers, and the whole thing will start again.

It's over! I've done it! I've gone on the Mountain Full of Monsters! I haven't written my full review yet, but it will go something like this:

12 THERE AND BACK AGAIN

I excitedly jump out of the car, ready to get back in line and do it all again. I quickly look around and then—

Out come Ricky and Becky, with the same blown-away look that I'm wearing . . . but no sign of Tina anywhere.

"Holy crud, Desmond!" Ricky says, grabbing me, his face the color of a cherry slushie. "What did we just go through?!"

"I know, right? Did you see the giant spider and graveyard of zombies and that crazy snow monster?!"

"And how about the exploding volcano!" Becky chimes in. "And the avalanche and the burning lake of fire!"

"I've got like a bajillion new ideas for my next Monster Magic event! Let's go on it again!"

"Well, maybe she'll see me on line. I'm going back in and this time I'm taking notes!"

"Nice hair, Needles!" laughs Principal Badonkus, who walks up from behind surprising us both. "Looks like you've been busy sharing a fun time with the children! What a team player! Good show!"

"Yes, news!" I jump in. "I have a great new idea for another Monster Magic show and Mr. Needles has been encouraging my creativity by taking me on the Mountain Full of Monsters ride!"

"Now just a second, Pucket—" sputters Mr. Needles.

"Yes! Another monster show!" booms Principal Badonkus. "Brilliant! That last one was such a success for the school it paid for this entire class trip! Keep it up, Needles!"

"Go on that Mountain Full of Monsters ride with Desmond as many times as you have to, Needles! You are making great strides forward in positive student-faculty relations! We're all counting on you! Well done, sir! Well done!"

Mr. Needles and I go on Mountain Full of Monsters nine more times. He stops screaming after the seventh time because he has no voice left. But I love every second!

OK, so the Mountain Full of Monsters ride doesn't go down *exactly* as I always dreamed . . .

But even with Mr. Needles next to me screaming and almost puking, it's a pretty amazing experience.

And the day isn't over yet! Mr. Needles is clearly suffering from coaster-overdose, so I leave him groaning on a bench near the Frozen Sour Gummy Worms stand. There's still time to get in one last Mountain Full of Monsters ride, and I start looking around for Tina.

And that's when I see the new sign . . .

13 THE BAD NEWS

"... if you want to know why the ride is closing, ask the guy who closes the rides!"

"So who's the guy who closes the rides?"

"Hey, what do I know, kid? Like I said—"

"Yeah, I know, I know. You're the guy who puts up the signs." *Note to self: if I ever need a sign guy, I know where to go.*

"I think you're catching on, kid," the sign guy says as he walks away. "But you might want to ask up at the pier management office . . ."

"You don't think they'd close the dunking tank, too, do you? That thing is my future dream job!"

And suddenly we're stopped dead in our tracks.

It's Tina Schimsky's best friend, Sheila Cutter! As usual, I'm completely flabbergasted whenever one of the popular kids talks to me. Or knows my first name, not to mention my last name, too!

"Who, me?"

"Yes, you! Tina was looking for you everywhere to go on that stupid monster ride! What happened?"

"Oh, I, uh . . ."

"He went on the ride ten times with Mr. Needles!" offers Ricky. "Mr. Needles has this special bracelet that lets them go to the front—"

"I had to go on the ride with Mr. Needles!" I explain. "Principal Badonkus was watching!"

"Yeah, I bet her dad had to come because she chickened out!" laughs Ricky. "Tina looked like she saw a ghost just standing in the line!"

"That's as much as you know, doofus!" Sheila shouts in Ricky's face. "She got sick!"

Sheila hands me a small piece of folded paper and walks away, totally ignoring the rude noises Ricky is making.

A note. A note from Tina Schimsky! To me!

I start to open the crinkled page when—

Not this time, Scott!

Like I always say: never leave home without extra rubber body parts and plenty of fake blood! And in a great diving play, Ricky grabs the note that Scott tossed.

Yeah, super-villain Scott Seltzer's one weakness: he's totally squeamish!

Once we're a safe distance from El Creepo, we stop running and Ricky hands me the note.

Hey, Desmond –

Sorry we didn't get to do the Mountain Full of Monsters ride together. I really wanted to! Next time for sure.

♡, Tina!

"Whoa," says Ricky who is reading over my shoulder. "Nice penmanship."

"Ricky, look at the heart . . . what do you think that means?"

"It means she likes you, dude!"

THEN I HAVE TO STOP THEM FROM CLOSING THE MOUNTAIN FULL OF MONSTERS!

UH, YEAH, OK...

". . . while you're making that happen, I'll be waiting for you back on planet Earth."

"I have to at least see why they're closing it, Ricky! Look, there's the management office . . ."

Suddenly I feel a tug on my shirt and my feet lift off the ground . . .

"No 'buts' this time, mister! I saw the blood and Scott Seltzer told me everything that happened!"

I turn around and see Scott laughing at me, fake blood all over his face!

"How lucky for you, Mr. Pucket! Now you'll have plenty of time to plot your next monster magic project in **Jug**! Principal Badonkus will be so pleased!"

14 JUG

"Jug" is short for the Latin word **jugum**, which means yoke, which is that giant wooden thing that goes on the cow's neck to pull a cart or a plow or something. But at Cloverfield Memorial Junior High, Jug has one meaning . . . "detention."

Or if you're me, it means hour after hour of sitting in one place while Scott Seltzer throws bits of whatever's in his pockets at your head.

Yeah, Scott's sitting Jug too, because we both got thrown out for fighting. But I know Scott doesn't care about missing the rest of the day at Crab Shell Pier.

It's been four hours in this hard seat, and I'm starting to lose the feeling in my butt. That's when I see Ricky in the hallway, waving for me. The class trip must be over!

I have this theory that the school punishes the lame teachers by making them sit with the kids who have to sit Jug. Which is why Mr. Turkle, the sleepiest teacher at Cloverfield, is usually in that chair.

"What . . . uh . . . Desmond Pucket, yes," Mr. Turkle says groggily, pawing at the attendance sheet. "What is it you are asking for?"

Good ol' Scott! He comes through again!

"Well, we can't have that," says Mr. Turkle, who sees Ricky through the narrow window of the door. Ricky suddenly notices Mr. Turkle looking and smiles. Then he does that imaginary elevator thing until he's out of sight.

"Hmmm . . . OK, yes, that sounds like an idea. Go together then, boys. And Scott, you make sure there's no dilly-dallying!"

That's my cue. I jump up and bolt through the door, shutting it behind me to put some space between me and Scott. The last thing I need is him reporting on my dilly-dallying.

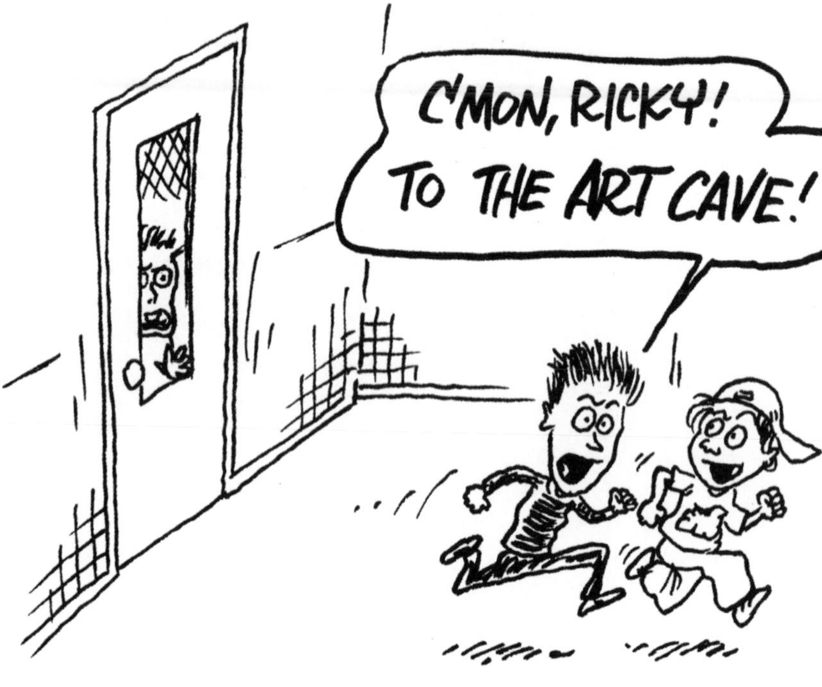
C'MON, RICKY! TO THE ART CAVE!

15 EVEN WORSE NEWS

When I was doing my week-long run of epic Monster Magic shows, I was allowed to go into the school art supply closet to get whatever I needed. The closet has this special keypad lock and everything, and Principal Badonkus personally gave me the code! Since then, it's sort of become my secret hideout.

Get it? Like the Bat Cave . . . only, like, with art stuff. OK, so maybe it is a stupid name. But until I come up with something better, that's what I call it, so deal!

And right now, the Art Cave is the perfect hiding spot for me and Ricky.

"I went into that management office trailer-thingie, and the guys in there told me the whole story! They bought a new super-fast roller coaster to replace your ride! Going to start building it after the summer! They showed me a model and everything!"

"But what are they going to do with the Mountain Full of Monsters?" I ask.

So much for my super-secret hideout.

"And I know all about it," boasts Scott. "Because it's my dad's company that's doing the blowing up! They're gonna put the bombs in, and then they're gonna set them off!"

Once again, Scott wants to take something that's mine. Only this time, he wants to blow it into a million pieces. I'll give him this: he thinks big!

Everybody in school knows Scott's dad works for a demolition company because, you have to admit, exploding stuff for a job is pretty cool.

So I'm kind of sure Scott's telling the truth, even the part about pushing the button to start the explosions! He's sort of a mini-celebrity because of it . . .

"This is going to be the most awesome one of all," giggles Scott. "I get to blow up Desmond's favorite plaything!"

Scott may get to push the button that blows up the Mountain Full of Monsters, but I still control the switches and pulleys in the Art Cave! And the shower of spiders and skulls sends him screaming back to the Jug room.

"Well, I guess that's that," says Ricky, sitting on a giant economy-size jar of paper paste. "Looks like there's no stopping the end of the Mountain Full of Monsters. At least we have it until the end of the summer."

Ricky's right. But then I start to get a tiny idea as I look at the skulls jouncing on their springs . . .

16 THE MONSTER FUND

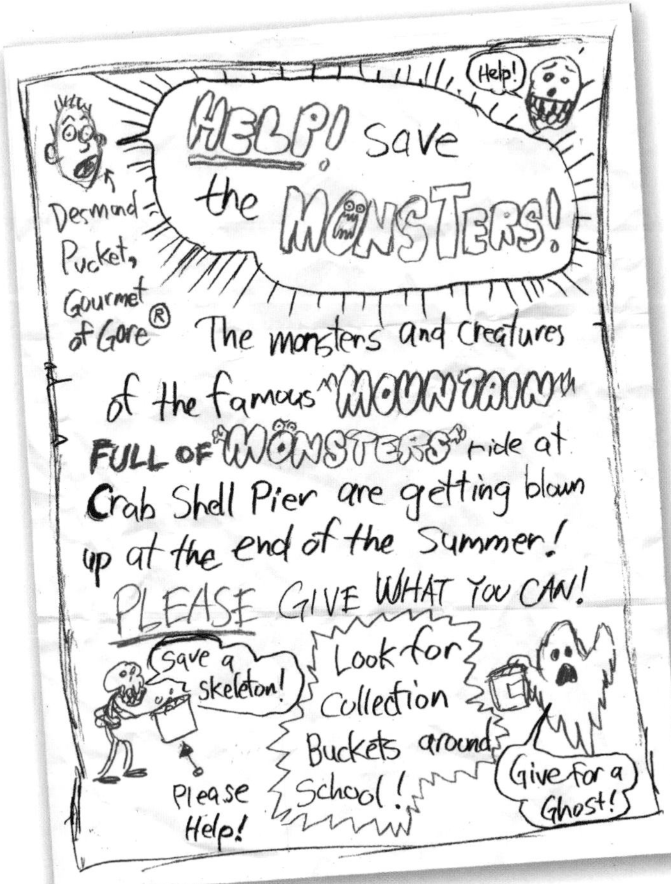

Help!
HELP! save the MONSTERS!
Desmond Pucket, Gourmet of Gore®
The monsters and creatures of the famous "MOUNTAIN FULL OF "MONSTERS" ride at Crab Shell Pier are getting blown up at the end of the Summer!
PLEASE GIVE WHAT YOU CAN!
Save a skeleton!
Look for Collection Buckets around School!
Please Help!
Give for a Ghost!

"They're going to let the monsters get blown up anyway, so what if I try to buy them? And when they see all the money, how can they say no?"

"You really think people are going to give you cash to save a bunch of ratty plastic monsters?" asks Becky, again looking at me like I spit in her ice cream sundae. "And just when I thought you couldn't out-weird yourself. Good luck, bro."

Becky has an odd way of calling me "genius," but I know what she means.

So Ricky and I get busy taping up flyers all over town and at school.

Then we sit back and wait to collect.

And wait.

And wait.

And wait.

All for a big fat nothing.

Well, that's not totally true. We did get one donation. From Mr. "Moneybags" Needles.

One penny. Hilarious.
And then I see Scott Seltzer at the end of the hall.

As far as worthy causes go that people want to give money to, "Save the Monsters" is pretty low on the importance scale.

But miracles always come in ways you least expect . . . and this time it's Tommy Templeton!

YOU'RE DESMOND PUCKET, RIGHT? THE KID WHO MADE THAT MONSTER MAGIC SHOW?

YEAH?

"That was really cool," Tommy continues. "And I heard about that awesome scare you gave your sister's slumber party. My sister Nadine was there and she still talks about it!"

"Well, I'm glad you're a fan!" I say, holding out the big empty bucket and jingling Mr. Needles's single penny. "Care to contribute to our 'Save the Monsters' fund?"

"Oh, I don't know," says Tommy, really thinking about it. "I would have to see what you plan to do first. But how's about maybe twenty bucks?"

"Twenty . . . *dollars*?!" I gasp excitedly. "Just to scare your kid brother?!"

I spin around and shake Ricky's leg.

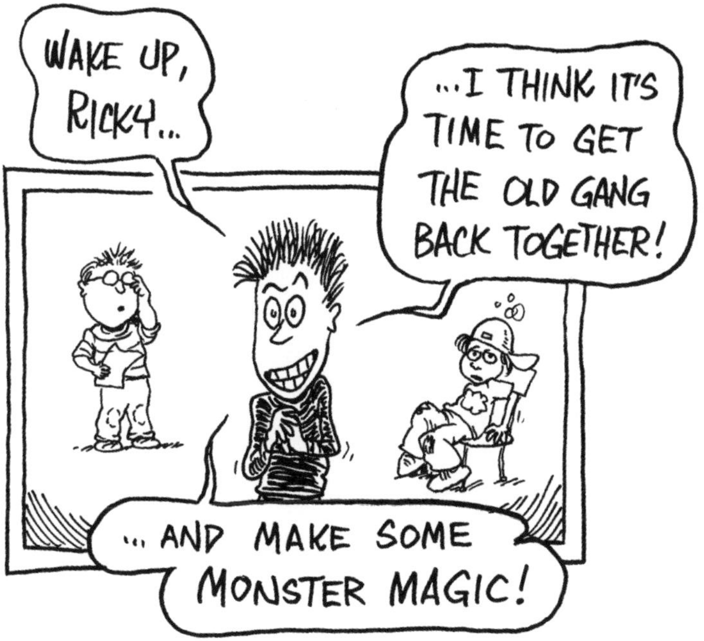
WAKE UP, RICKY...
...I THINK IT'S TIME TO GET THE OLD GANG BACK TOGETHER!
...AND MAKE SOME MONSTER MAGIC!

17 BACK TO THE MAGIC

Of course, getting the old gang back together isn't as easy as I think . . .

Today is the last day of school and it looks like everybody already has summer plans. The Wickerstool twins are all wrapped up in their new classics reading group; Becky is being a weird girl (though I'm pretty sure that's not a summer thing . . . I don't know what planet she's on these days); and Ricky is . . . well . . . just Ricky. Clown School? Really?

So I grab my overstuffed spiral notebook of super scary monster effects and gross ideas, and I get to work planning the first scare of my new business.

A "window scare" is when you can't actually get in the house, and in this case Tommy says inside is off-limits. So all the frights have to happen at the outside windows. And the more windows, the more screams!

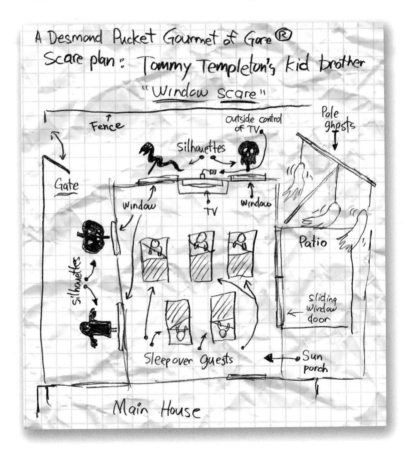

This scare is pretty simple. Still, it's tricky to pull off by myself. But I can do it! First, I turn their TV to static with an outdoor remote control. Then I start making sounds outside so they'll all begin looking out the windows . . . and that's when the fun begins. I just run from window to window with silhouette cutouts of monsters, lighting them up from behind with my Hollywood-grade studio flashlight. And then finally, to the back patio for the three pole ghosts that—

Dang! I'm so wrapped up in my plans that Mom snuck right up on me! I hope she didn't see my work.

It won't be good if she finds out I was scaring for money . . . especially if she tells Dad.

"So I was wondering why on such a beautiful sunny day my son is inside," Mom says in that all-knowing mom voice. "I should've figured you were planning your next scare-fest."

Yeah, that's just what an eleven-year-old wants to hear. That he used to wear diapers. Thanks, Mom!

"Please don't tell Dad, OK, Mom?"

"Aw, c'mon, I won't tell . . . who do I look like, Mr. Needles?"

Mom's starting to win back some points.

"I don't mind your hobby, Desmond. As long as nobody gets hurt, it's fine with me. I think you're really creative, and that's always a good thing!"

"Well, it's still early," she says. "I'm sure they'll come back around. At the very least, this summer will be a nice break from Mr. Needles, right?"

But Mom is already gone, shutting the door behind her. That was weird . . . what did she mean by that?

Oh, well, whatever. It's getting late and I have to finish getting ready for the scare tonight.

I put the final touches on the master plan. Then I gather up all my monster silhouettes, tuck them in my magic bag of tricks, grab my night-vision goggles, and head for the door to make my way to Tommy Templeton's house.

Once again, I get that excited/scared feeling in the pit of my stomach that I know means only one thing . . .

18 SCARING FOR DOLLARS

It's a quiet, cool summer night and the streets are empty. I carefully make my way through the neighborhood, ducking in and out of the shadows.

I'm really good at ducking in and out of shadows. If I wasn't so into monsters, shadow-ducking would be my second career choice.

The houses on Decatur Lane all sort of look the same, especially in the dark. I reach into my bag of tricks for a small flashlight and a scrap of paper.

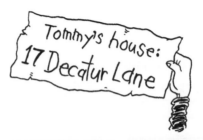

I switch over to my night-vision goggles and start scanning the mailboxes for house numbers.

"Hot dog, there it is!" I whisper to myself as I dart across the street toward the Templeton house.

I feel my way down the boards of the tall fence . . .

. . . the gate is unlocked, just like Tommy said!

I duck into the shadow of the bushes (see, again with the ducking into shadows, because, like I said, I'm a total expert) and I peer out at the small sun porch where the sleepover is happening.

Now the boring part. The sitting and waiting for the lights to go out. But Tommy said that should be in about an hour, and he's been right so far. So I settle down with my new issue of *Hugo the Boy Zombie Wizard* and wait.

Ten. Thirty. Fifty minutes pass. And then ping!

It's showtime! I pull out the silhouettes and ready the turbo flashlight. Hopefully Tommy got the pole ghosts into position like he said he would. I start to crawl out from the darkness of the bushes.

And suddenly, I hear a snort. Then a deep, low, rumbling ggggrrrrrrrrrrrrrrrrowwwwwwwllllllll.

And I'm absolutely sure I would have remembered if good ol' Tommy said something about . . .

That's a bad detail to leave out.

Don't get me wrong, I love dogs. And normally they love me.

So I squeeze up into a tight ball and get ready to be ripped apart. Though, seriously, can you really prepare for that?

And just like that, the dogs are gone! Disappeared! For a second I think maybe they were never really there. But no, I can still smell their doggie breath. Just no doggies!

"Sheesh, boy! You don't know nothing about handling no hound dogs, do you?"

"Good thing we showed up when we did! Look that way to you, Jessup?"

"And how, Jasper! They was about to turn him into little bitty Desmond meatballs!"

"Ricky! What—" I gasp.

"Aw, your Mom called my grandma because she was worried about you," Ricky says, rolling his eyes. "And I called everybody else."

"Everybody?" I ask.

"All right, y'all, let's be honest now . . . we all know the real tar that holds this old row boat together . . . "

"Enough with the love-fest, already," says Becky. "There's a bunch of creepy nine-year-olds in there waiting to get the snot scared out of 'em!"

19 A BLOODCURDLING BUSINESS BLOOMS

I don't care what kind of social networking you think is the best, nothing tops the big mouth of Tommy Templeton.

And it isn't long before our little scare business is booming!

Suddenly kids from everywhere are running up to me on the street or in the store to ask about my spooky services.

No matter how much money they have, I can find a scare that works for their price. And we have different frights for different ages: "Kiddie Kreepy" (ages 5–7, pretty tame), "Middle Monster Mayhem" (ages 8–13, scary), and "The Dr. Shock" (14 and up, full-blast, in-your-kitchen horror). We haven't pulled out "The

Dr. Shock" yet, and I'm almost afraid for anyone to ask!

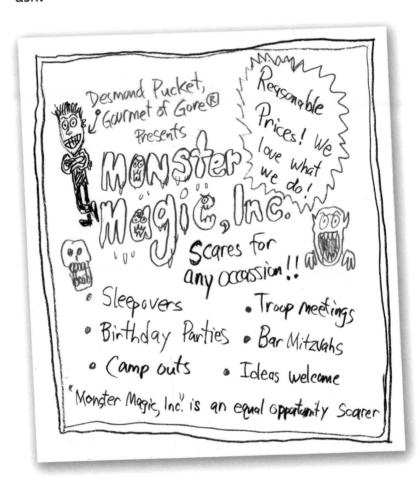

When the Wickerstool twins print this ad in their neighborhood newsletter, things really go crazy and we realize we're definitely going to need an extra set of claws.

Ding dong!

"I'll get it," I yell from behind the mound of monster ideas piled on my desk.

"It's not me, though," Tina says quickly.

"Oh," I say, trying not to look like my whole world was just crushed like a soda can. "I didn't think—"

If I were wearing a set of fangs, I definitely would have swallowed them.

"Desmond, meet Keith, a big fan . . . and my kid brother."

HA HA HA HA HA! THAT WAS AWESOME! YOU SHOULD'VE SEEN YOUR FACE!

"Well, haha, good one, Keith," I say, hoping nobody notices that I almost pooped myself. "Nice to meet you . . . I think."

"He's so excited, Desmond! When I heard you were looking for another monster for your team, I immediately thought of him."

"I even have all my own masks and everything! And I'm already kind of a pro! My specialty is scaring little kids and really old people!"

"Congratulations, Keith! You're hired!"

"Gosh, thanks, Mr. Desmond! Let's shake!"

Yeah, the master didn't even see it coming! But that's OK, because the kid seems to know what he's doing. And I need him! We've got a million and two scares lined up and it's already the end of June! Time is running out on the Mountain Full of Monsters!

20 SUMMER FULL OF SCREAMS

OK, I'm no math wiz, but by my calculations, every scream we get is worth about twelve cents. And the screams are really piling up!

The Anderwood sisters' birthday pays off big time. That's a daylight scare with twenty partygoers, so the effects have to be big and dramatic! Keith Schimsky's dad is a house painter, so he has these really awesome strap-on stilts. So I borrow them . . .

. . . and enter *The Towering Beast from Behind the Shed*! Yes! Another successful backyard fright-fest!

And then there's the Graduation Spider Cake . . .

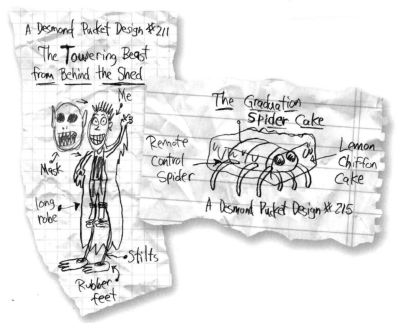

. . . a really cool design with this remote control spider–robot baked into a cake. The legs burst out through the icing and the whole cake creeps off across the table!

It's awesome! More screams! More bucks!

And the hits keep on coming!

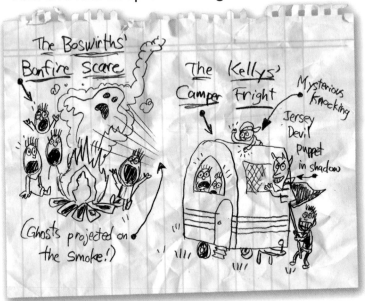

The bride was not amused.

Of course, the big surprise this summer is Tina Schimsky's brother, Keith! He is a great addition to the Monster Magic team. Most of the new ideas are his, though I have to keep the kid under control.

Yeah, Keith's pretty sharp about the scare ideas, but I'm definitely going to have to keep an eye on him.

Anyway, it's the third week in July and we've raised a bucket of dough to save the monsters!

I think I'm ready to make my offer!

Now I just need to find a ride back to Crab Shell Pier . . .

21 THE BUS KID

My sister Rachel doesn't drive, but her boyfriend Kyle does. Which means after I'm done begging Rachel to let Kyle give me a ride, I have to deal with Kyle. And dealing with Kyle usually means . . .

As you can see, Kyle and Rachel have a lot in common. Their annoyingness is off the charts.

I would ask Mom or Dad for a ride, but the last thing I need them to know is I'm planning on buying all the creatures from the Mountain Full of Monsters. So I'm stuck with Kyle. Or as we all know him:

KYLE THE BUS KID

Rachel's weird boyfriend

one of many bus T-shirts

an actual bus belt buckle, I kid you not.

Long hair, an important part of any Rachel boyfriend

Colored Jeans, usually red. Need I say more?

Yes, you heard right . . . Kyle the bus kid. Some people collect action figures, some people love sneakers . . . this kid is totally and completely into buses. All kinds of buses. Passenger buses. School buses. Double-decker and flexi-middle city buses. You name the bus, and Kyle can tell you all about it.

And Kyle drives this big clunky van, which I think is from The Land Before Time. It's also the closest thing he could find to an actual bus.

Believe it or not, I actually like Kyle when he isn't being a noodge. I can totally understand a guy who's into something that most people think is pretty weird.

Of course, it's hard for me to like him right now, when his armpit is in my face.

We pile into the van (Ricky and Becky are coming, too) and we sit facing each other in a space that looks like some crazy person's living room exploded.

Kyle starts the van with a roar, Pink Floyd rock music blasting from the speakers, and screeches away from the curb. Somewhere, I know my Dad is groaning.

But I wouldn't even care if we were driving with Mr. Needles in a clown car . . .

. . . we're heading back to The Crab and we're going to rescue some monsters!

22 MAKING A MONSTER DEAL

I never actually saw someone laugh until he choked before. And if I never see it again, that will totally be OK. Especially if it's Mr. Humphries doing the laughing and choking.

Mr. Humphries is the manager of Crab Shell Pier, and his little trailer office is filled with old amusement park pictures and old amusement park food smells.

The boxy room has windows, but they look like they've never been opened. And Mr. Humphries looks like a guy who's been sitting in a little room with unopened windows for years and years.

"So let me get this straight," he says between the laughs and coughs. "You kids want to buy the monsters from the Mountain Full of Monsters ride?!"

YOU'RE GOING TO BLOW THEM UP ANYWAY... WHY NOT MAKE SOME MONEY?! AND I'VE GOT $374.74 TO GIVE THE MONSTERS A NEW HOME!

I used to have $414.74, but I had to give Kyle the bus kid $20 for gas. And $20 went to Rachel for "boyfriend rental." I kid you not.

And then, more laughing and choking.

"Are you for real, kid?! I wouldn't blow those things up! Those old pieces of crud are worth thousands!"

". . . he's coming to pick them up this weekend," finishes Mr. Humphries.

I just stand there in shock. The only sound in the room is Mr. Humphries's straw as he sucks the last drops out of his Colossa-Cola. Finally, Kyle the bus kid breaks the silence.

My heart sinks. We all start to slowly move out of the tiny trailer office. But I can't let it go that easily.

"*No!*" I shout. "No! They're ***not*** just stupid monsters!"

Now I'm right in Mr. Humphries's face, but he just stares back at me with a blank look in his eyes. I sigh and head for the door, waving to the others.

"Let's get out of here, guys. He just doesn't—"

"*Stop!*" yells Mr. Humphries. "Wait . . ."

"Come back on Saturday, before the junk man. I'll let you and your friends in the Mountain Full of Monsters. You can take whatever monsters you can haul off. For $500 bucks. That's the best I can do."

I shake hands with Mr. Humphries and my mind is already racing, trying to figure how to pull this off.

"And you're right, Desmond," Mr. Humphries says as he turns and reaches for one of the old faded photos, pulling it off the wall. "Those monsters are a piece of history."

He looks at the picture for a moment and then hands it to me.

"I love them as much as you do."

CRAB SHELL PIER

Benji Humphries, age Nine— The Mountain full of monsters

23 DESMOND THE IDIOTIC

"I have no idea what's going on in that avocado-size brain of yours," Rachel says as soon as we get back in the van. "Where are you going to get the rest of that money?! And don't even think for a second that Kyle is driving you back here on Saturday, because he's not! Guh, you're such an idiot!"

"I hate to say it, dude, but she's right . . ."

"Well, we can't give up now," I say. "There must be something we haven't thought of!"

"No, Dumbo," says Becky. "Tina's having a huge all-night birthday party campout at Cloverfield Park this Friday! Every girl in the entire sixth grade is invited. I'm invited, too!"

SO? SHE'S HAVING A BIRTHDAY CAMPOUT! ARE WE GOING TO RENT THEM SLEEPING BAGS?

NO, BUT I BET THERE ARE LOTS OF BROTHERS AND SISTERS WHO WOULD PAY US SOMETHING TO **SCARE** THOSE SIXTH GRADERS!

"Becky, that's an incredibly awesome idea," I start. "But, the only problem is . . ."

"Oh, brother, here we go," Becky says, her eyes rolling like crazy.

". . . nothing too crazy! We'll keep it a 'Fun Scare,' OK?"

OK. BECKY, YOU AND RICKY HEAD OUT AND FIND BROTHERS, SISTERS, AUNTS, UNCLES...

... ANYBODY THAT'S WILLING TO PAY ANYTHING FOR THIS...

". . . meanwhile, the Wickerstool twins, Keith, and I will plan and put together *The Great Summer Campout Scare of Cloverfield Park!*"

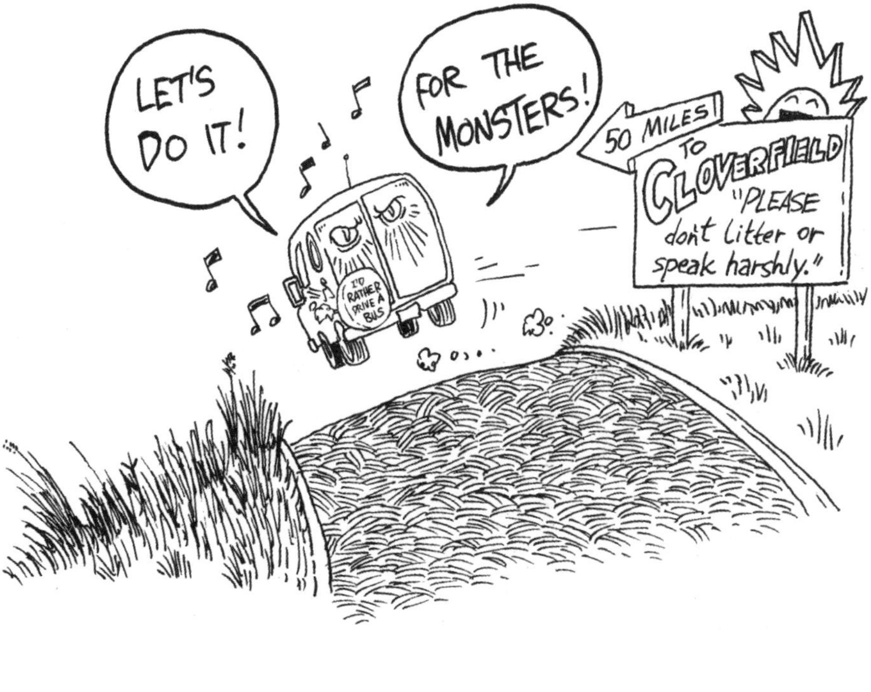
LET'S DO IT!
FOR THE MONSTERS!
I'D RATHER DRIVE A BUS
50 MILES
TO CLOVERFIELD
"PLEASE don't litter or speak harshly."

24 THE PLAN

"You must chill, Keith! You're going to give the scare-biz a bad name!"

"But . . . " Keith says, "we'll be in the woods . . . in the middle of the night . . . lots of girls sitting around a fire telling ghost stories . . . surrounded by total darkness . . ."

NO, KEITH! NOT THIS TIME! NOT FOR YOUR SISTER'S PARTY!
BESIDES, I ALREADY CAME UP WITH A SPECIAL PLAN!

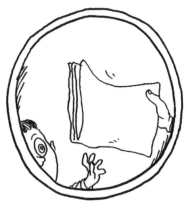

Top
Secret

The Great Summer Campout Scare
of Cloverfield Park®   A Desmond Pucket
Master Plan®

Top
Secret

harness in tree

Jessup

tents

Ghost Army

Me,
The
Winged
Vampire
dude

1) Sixth grade
   girls around
   fire
2) tell Ghost
   Stories
3) Scary sounds

4) Ghosts surround

5) I fly in as winged
   Vampire dude and
   rescue Tina

"And here's the best part, Keith . . . you're in charge of the ghosts! We had to hire a bunch of extra kids, and **you're** going to make sure they scare when they're supposed to scare!"

". . . how does that sound?"

"It sounds really lame," says Keith.

"OK, look, I know it's not the greatest. But this scare is going to pay to save the monsters from Crab Shell Pier!"

"Come on, Keith . . . we really need this to go off without a hitch. Right after the scare, we have to head straight to Crab Shell Pier before the junk man comes . . ."

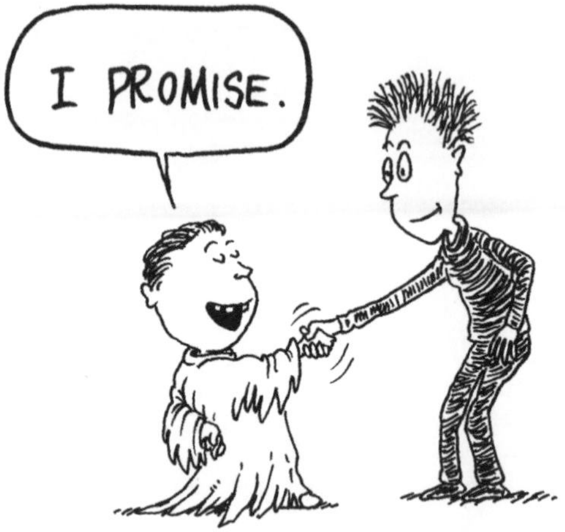
I PROMISE.

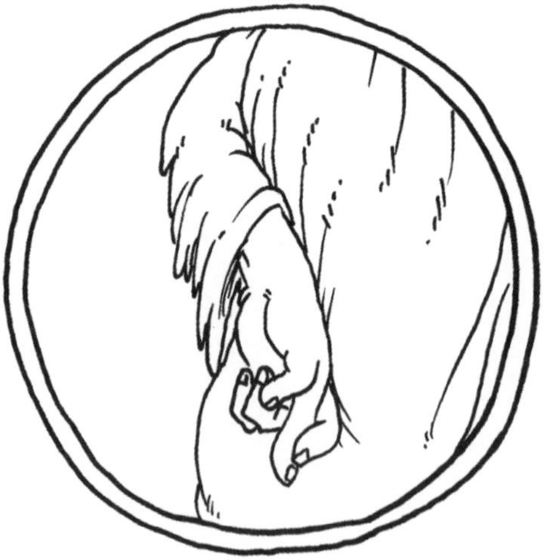

25 THE GREAT SUMMER CAMPOUT SCARE OF CLOVERFIELD PARK

Everything is in place and ready to go. The team is just waiting for my signal. From my tree position high above the campsite, I bend the communications microphone toward my mouth.

Becky rigged the trees yesterday with a boatload of wireless mini-speakers . . .

. . . and Ricky's off in the bushes with the remote that will launch his prerecorded moans and groans and howls (and no doubt, the occasional atomic fart . . . it's his trademark!).

Becky is our "inside person" . . . actually down there mixed in with the sixth grade girls sitting around the roaring bonfire, though she's not linked into our ear bud walkie-talkies.

She just has a small flashlight to signal me when the ghost-storytelling hits the perfect point at which to start the campout scare.

Any minute now.

Any second—

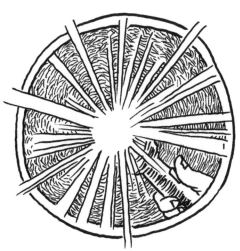

Right on cue, Ricky's creepy soundtrack of monsters and ghosts and farts fills the dark woods surrounding the crowd of girls. The constant chatter and laughing below me comes to a quick stop as the eerie sounds grow louder, weirder, and fartier.

And then . . .
Nothing.

I bang my microphone and try again. Still nothing.

And then . . .

Suddenly, crashing through the bushes and trees toward the mass of screaming, scrambling girls . . .

. . . *an army of giant crazy killer clowns with chainsaws!* Keith Schimsky executed an unauthorized "Dr. Shock"!

I have to admit, these freaky clown monsters are amazing! I'll have to find out how Keith pulled it off! But right now, I have to stop this before it gets any more out of control . . .

With a sharp tug on the harness that he and Jasper had rigged, Jessup blasts me up and over the wild scene.

I hit the ground and start looking for one person . . .

I run up and grab his shoulder, spinning him around
to face me.

Keith Schimsky's laugh cuts through all the noise of
crazy chainsaw clowns and screaming sixth grade girls.

"You're finished, Pucket! Washed up! Done!"

Before I can say anything, whistles and shouts add to the mess of noise. Searchlights sweep through the trees.

"Park rangers!" growls Keith, and dives into the shadows.

I turn to run, and in the chaos I crash right into the last person I want to see right now.

"No, no, wait! You don't understand! It wasn't me! I tried—"

Suddenly whistles, flashlights, and footsteps are all around us. The park rangers are closing in! I make a move for the shadows but—

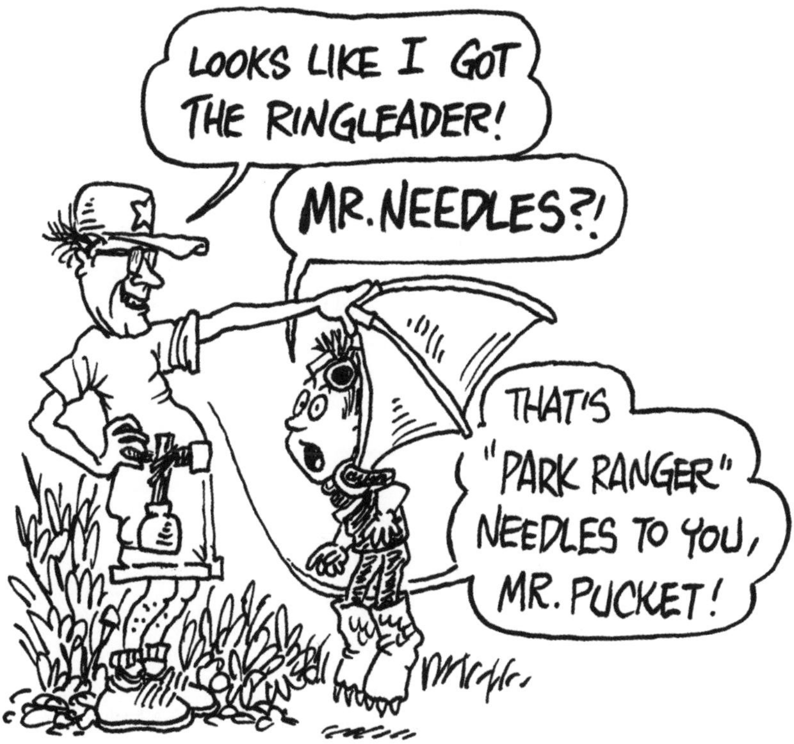
LOOKS LIKE I GOT THE RINGLEADER!
MR. NEEDLES?!
THAT'S "PARK RANGER" NEEDLES TO YOU, MR. PUCKET!

26 EXPLOSION IN MY FACE

Did you ever wonder where teachers go during the summer? Do they have other jobs? Are they put into suspended animation? Are they released into the wild?

I just figured after the last day of school, Mr. Needles went back into storage—

So nice to return to my natural home! Wake me when the sun is gone!

Count Needles

It makes total sense that Mr. Needles, the school disciplinarian, would be a park ranger: he can be much more annoying with a flashlight and a whistle.

Seated in the little park ranger guard house, Mr. Needles wastes no time jumping all over me.

WELL, WELL. MR. PUCKET... HOW STRANGE FOR US TO MEET IN THE SUMMER. AND THIS TIME YOU'RE REALLY IN TROUBLE!

"Not only did you violate numerous Cloverfield Park rules, but you personally ruined Miss Schimsky's birthday campout! What a shame! I know you've been sweet on her for months!"

For once, Mr. Needles is right. And when my Dad hears all this, I'll be grounded for a million years and I won't be able to make it to Crab Shell Pier in time and the monsters will get sold to that junk dealer. Not that I had a way to get back there anyway, because Rachel won't let her boyfriend drive me . . .

All I wanted to do was save some old monsters from getting blown up . . . and the whole thing ended up exploding in my face.

To quote a favorite cartoon character, "That's all I can stands, I can stands no more!" Now if I only had some spinach, and that spinach could turn me into a super-human sailor with giant forearms, I'd go all Popeye on Mr. Needles! Instead, I jump onto the table and—

WHAT'S YOUR PROBLEM, MR. NEEDLES?! WHAT DID I EVER DO TO YOU?! WHY DO YOU HATE ME SO MUCH?!

"I thought school officials are supposed to try to help the students," I scream. "All you ever do is try to get me in trouble! What do you have against me?!"

Suddenly the room grows quiet and Mr. Needles stands with his back to me.

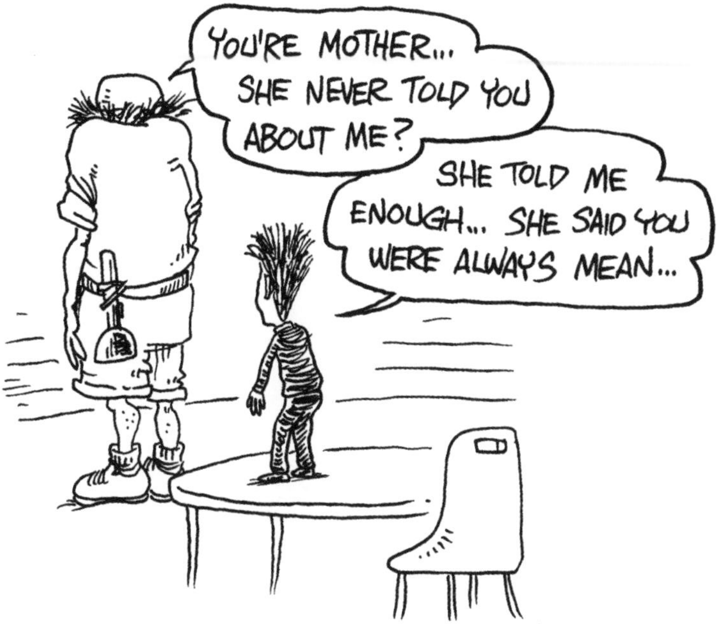
YOU'RE MOTHER... SHE NEVER TOLD YOU ABOUT ME?
SHE TOLD ME ENOUGH... SHE SAID YOU WERE ALWAYS MEAN...

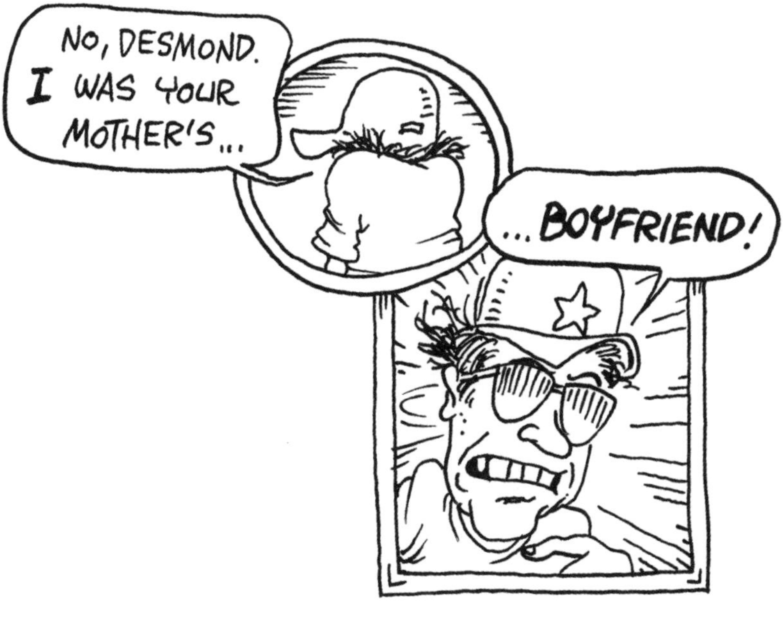
NO, DESMOND. I WAS YOUR MOTHER'S...
...BOYFRIEND!

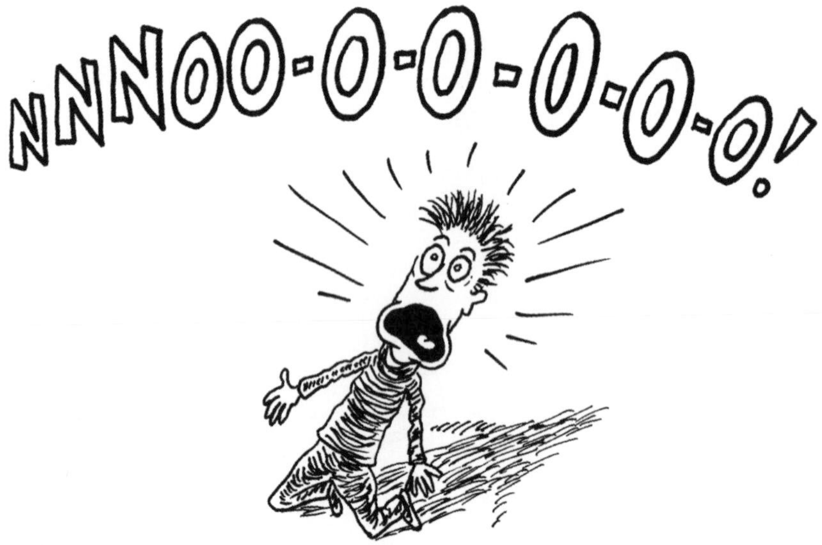
NNNOO-O-O-O-O-O!

27 YES!

"Search your feelings, Desmond!" Mr. Needles says in a low voice. "You know it to be true!"

Whoa! I'm totally having a weird Darth Vader/Luke Skywalker moment here.

YOUR MOTHER WAS MY GIRLFRIEND AND YOUR FATHER CAME ALONG AND RUINED EVERYTHING! AND NOW YOU'RE JUST LIKE HIM IN EVERY WAY!

?

"Hang on a second, Mr. Needles . . . are we talking about the same father . . . who's my dad?"

"Well, he's not like you now, Desmond, but he used to be," says Mr. Needles.

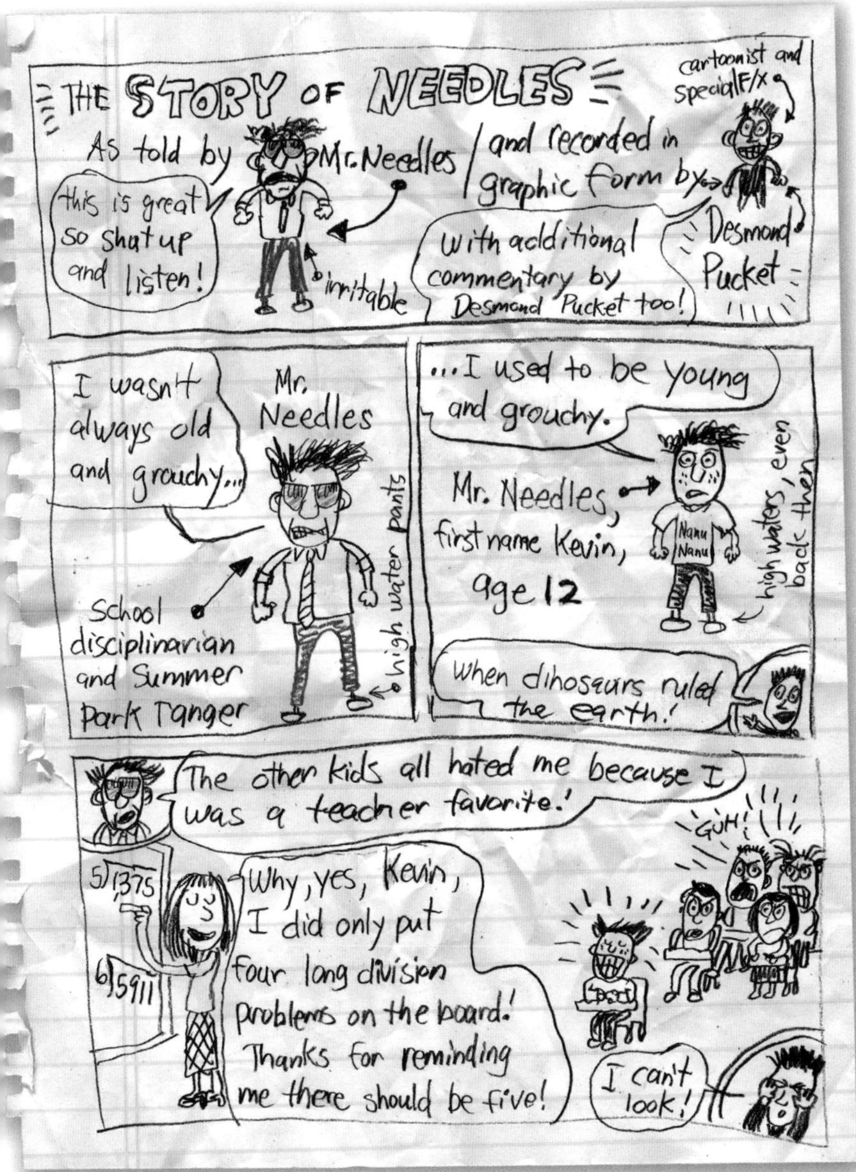
THE STORY OF NEEDLES
As told by Mr. Needles
this is great so shut up and listen!
irritable
and recorded in graphic form by
cartoonist and special F/X
Desmond Pucket
with additional commentary by Desmond Pucket too!
I wasn't always old and grouchy...
Mr. Needles
School disciplinarian and Summer Park ranger
high water pants
...I used to be young and grouchy.
Mr. Needles, first name Kevin, age 12
Nanu Nanu
high waters, even back then
When dinosaurs ruled the earth!
The other kids all hated me because I was a teacher favorite!
5)1375
6)5911
Why, yes, Kevin, I did only put four long division problems on the board! Thanks for reminding me there should be five!
GUH!
I can't look!

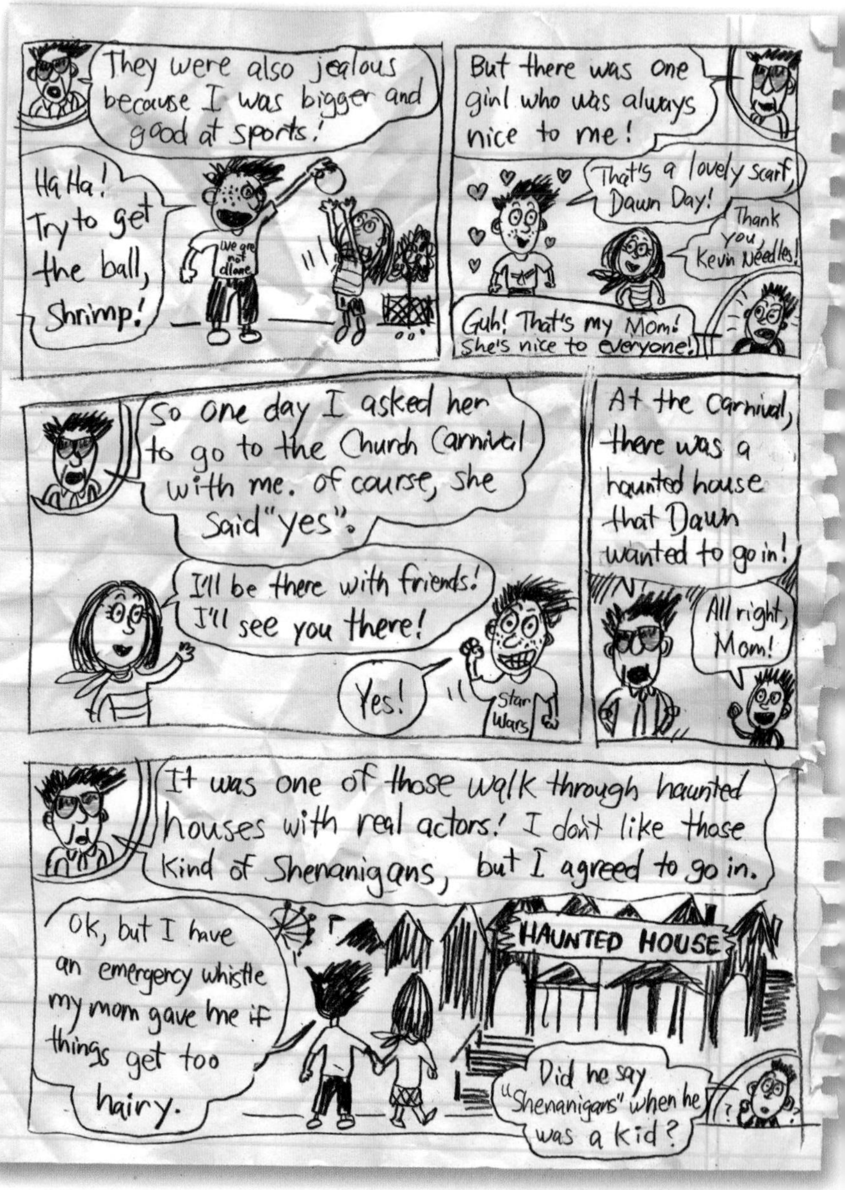
They were also jealous because I was bigger and good at sports!
Ha Ha! Try to get the ball, Shrimp!
We are not alone
But there was one girl who was always nice to me!
That's a lovely scarf, Dawn Day!
Thank you, Kevin Needles!
Guh! That's my Mom! She's nice to everyone!
So one day I asked her to go to the Church Carnival with me. of course, she said "yes".
I'll be there with friends! I'll see you there!
Yes!
Star Wars
At the Carnival, there was a haunted house that Dawn wanted to go in!
All right, Mom!
It was one of those walk through haunted houses with real actors! I don't like those kind of Shenanigans, but I agreed to go in.
Ok, but I have an emergency whistle my mom gave me if things get too hairy.
HAUNTED HOUSE
Did he say "Shenanigans" when he was a kid?

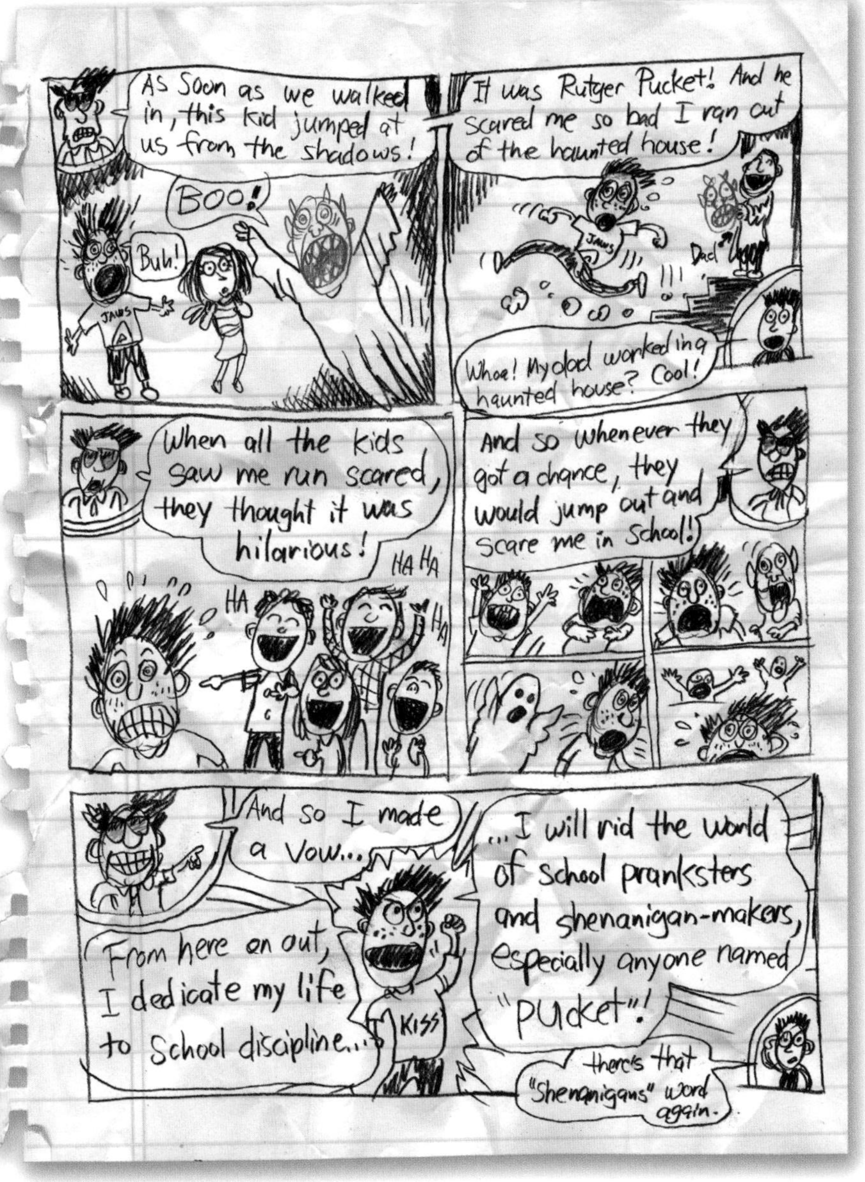
As Soon as we walked in, this kid jumped at us from the shadows!
BOO!
Buh!
JAWS
It was Rutger Pucket! And he scared me so bad I ran out of the haunted house!
JAWS
Dad
Whoa! My dad worked in a haunted house? Cool!
When all the kids saw me run scared, they thought it was hilarious!
HA HA
HA
HA
And so whenever they got a chance, they would jump out and scare me in School!
And so I made a vow...
...I will rid the world of School pranksters and shenanigan-makers, especially anyone named "Pucket"!
From here on out, I dedicate my life to School discipline...
KISS
there's that "Shenanigans" word again.

"So you see, Desmond, you Puckets are all alike! And I will not rest until you and your shenanigans are expunged from all parks and recreation areas!"

AND WHEN SCHOOL STARTS AGAIN, WITH THESE NEW CHARGES IN HAND, I WILL ONCE AGAIN PUSH FOR YOUR IMMEDIATE EXPULSION!

Wow, that's a lot of big important words. And even "shenanigans" and "expunged" stuck in one sentence too!

I suppose when you "dedicate your life to school discipline."

... the first thing they do is teach you scary words that only disciplinarians are allowed to use.

Suddenly a bright beam of car headlights flashes across the wooden walls of the small park cabin and Mr. Needles smiles devilishly.

"And that should be your parents now . . ."

. . . as crazy as this night has been, and now as it ends with me getting grounded and losing the Crab Shell Pier monsters forever . . . I still can't get used to the idea of Mom and Mr. Needles holding hands, or Dad working in a carnival haunted house! Even if it was a hundred years ago!

We hear the car getting closer.

And closer. And closer . . .

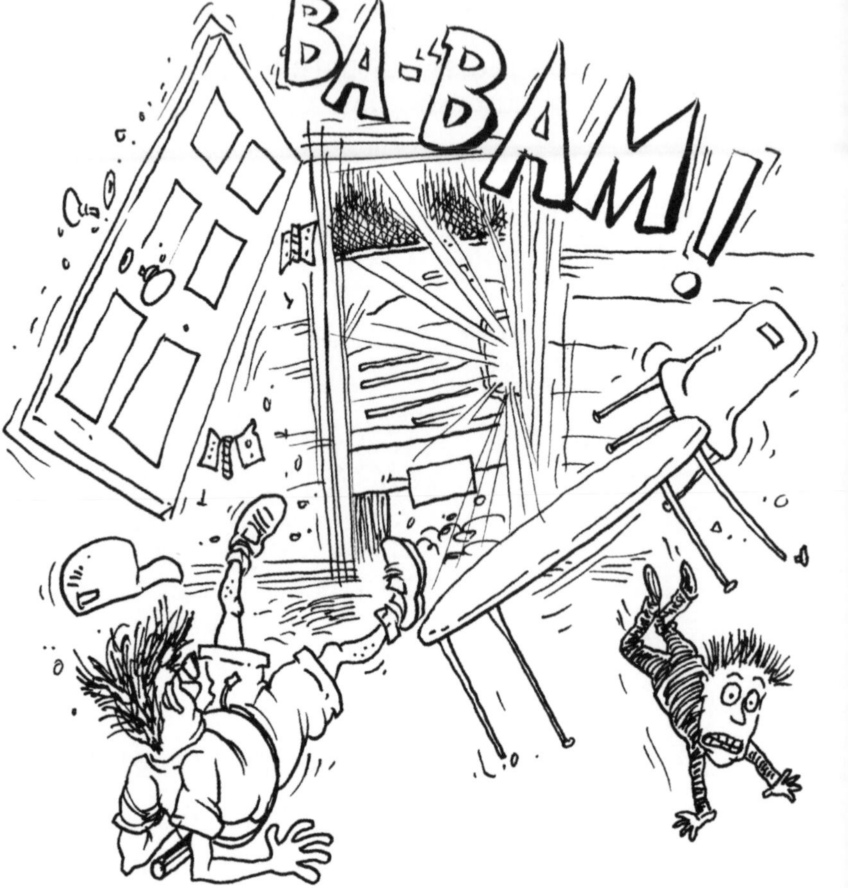
BA-BAM!

28 THE BRAVE LITTLE RESCUE

"Desmond, come on!"

It's Ricky! Without even thinking, I jump up and head to the doorway that no longer has its door.

"Is that even a thing?" I ask, as I yank my foot away from Mr. Needles's tight grip.

I follow Ricky outside and . . . what do I hear? **Christmas music?!**

"But how—," I ask in amazement.

"Becky did it, Desmond," Ricky says as he hurries me to the vehicle. "When things fell apart at the scare, we all scattered and then met up at my house!"

"But who's driving?" I ask as Ricky pulls me through the door.

"*Woo hoo!* You think I'd ever turn down a chance to drive a '53 Volvo 638 bus?!" screams Kyle the bus kid, happy as a clam behind the wheel.

I look around the bus and everybody's here: Ricky, Becky, the Wickerstool twins, and even Ricky's grandparents (who greet me with the usual "Merry Christmas, Desmond!"). But judging from the look on my sister's face . . .

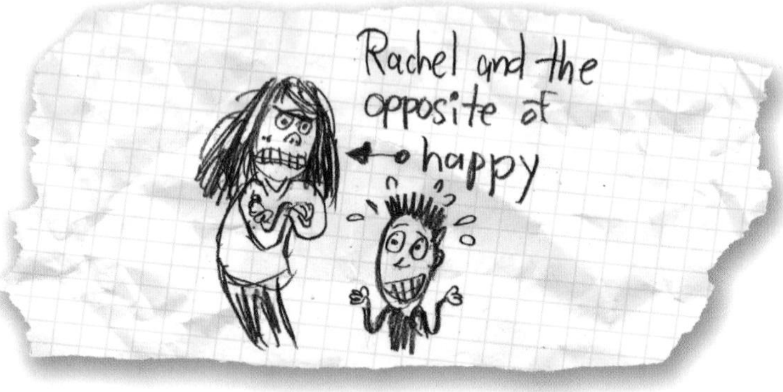
Rachel and the opposite of happy

. . . the last place she wants to be this very early Saturday morning is in a '53 Volvo 638 *Santa Express* bus.

Suddenly we hear a bunch of loud blasts from a whistle. I quickly look out the window.

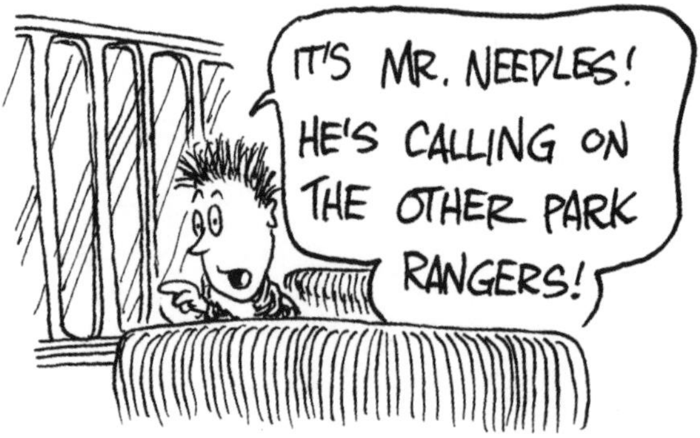
IT'S MR. NEEDLES! HE'S CALLING ON THE OTHER PARK RANGERS!

"Then it's time to blow this popsicle stand," says Kyle as he pulls the bus door closed and revs the jittery engine.

Kyle throws the bus into gear and it lurches onto the road with great fits and jerks, belching smoke as it slowly ramps up to speed.

Becky smiles and sits back. And then I start to see her in a way I never have before. Suddenly Becky's not just the kid who's good with a wrench and a left hook, but somebody who always comes through when I need her most. Somebody who—

Then I hear noise from the very last seat of the bus . . .

"Who's back there?" I ask Becky.

"Oh, yeah, little Miss Perfect," Becky replies with a roll of her eyes. "She decided to tag along."

I stand and walk to the back of the rocking bus. I don't believe it. Tina Schimsky.

"Well, I'm really sorry, Desmond . . . I feel like I dumped him on you in the first place."

"Actually, I like Keith, Tina! He's really smart and knows his monster stuff! He just has to remember to scare for *fun* . . . not for meanness."

"Behind us! It's Mr. Needles! And a gang of his park rangers on scooters! Right on our tail!"

"I'll try to go faster, Desmond," shouts Kyle. "But this old bus is giving us everything she's got!"

"They're closing in," I gasp.

"If they force us off the road, we'll never get to Crab Shell Pier!"

Meanwhile, I see Ricky's grandparents struggling with something under one of the back seats.

"Relax, Desmond, dear," says Mrs. DiMarco, patting my hand. "With all this worrying, you're going to give yourself the diarrhea!"

Suddenly, Mr. DiMarco throws open the back window of the bus.

"Mr. DiMarco, be careful!" I shout.

"Relax, kid! I've done this a million times!"

Then it dawns on me: I've seen that big white tube before . . . and the black machine they pulled out from under the seat. Ricky hits the "on" switch and a blizzard of white starts pumping out the back window of the bus.

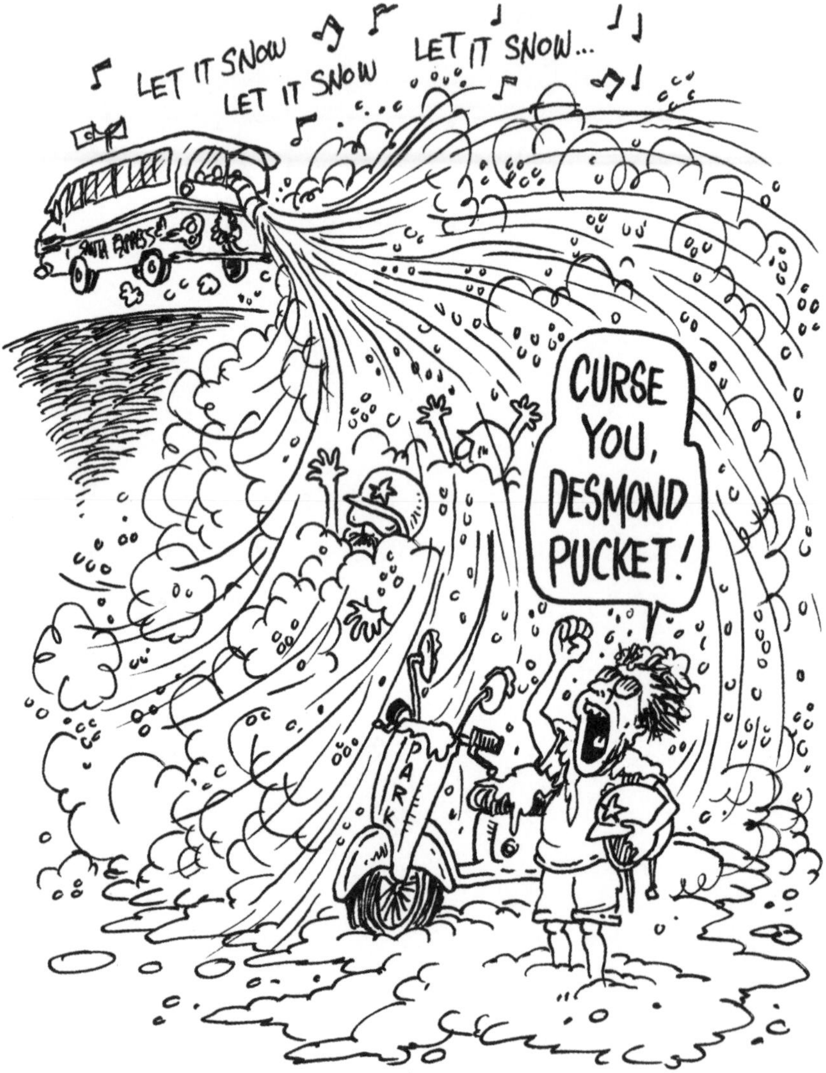
LET IT SNOW
LET IT SNOW
LET IT SNOW...
CURSE YOU, DESMOND PUCKET!
PARK

29 RETURN TO CRAB SHELL PIER

The sun is just starting to rise as we pull up to Crab Shell Pier. Mr. Humphries is out front waiting.

"I figured I was going to have to let the junk dealer clean out everything from the Mountain Full of Monsters!"

"We almost *didn't* make it," I say, as I hand Mr. Humphries the $500. "And you can read all about it in my memoirs. But for now, let's see those monsters!"

Everyone piles out of the bus and follows Mr. Humphries as he leads us down the boardwalk, filing past the rows of quiet rides. There's always something sad about walking around a closed amusement park. Like seeing a bunch of giant toys waiting patiently for the kids to come back and play with them.

"I know, Mr. Humphries, but don't worry . . ."

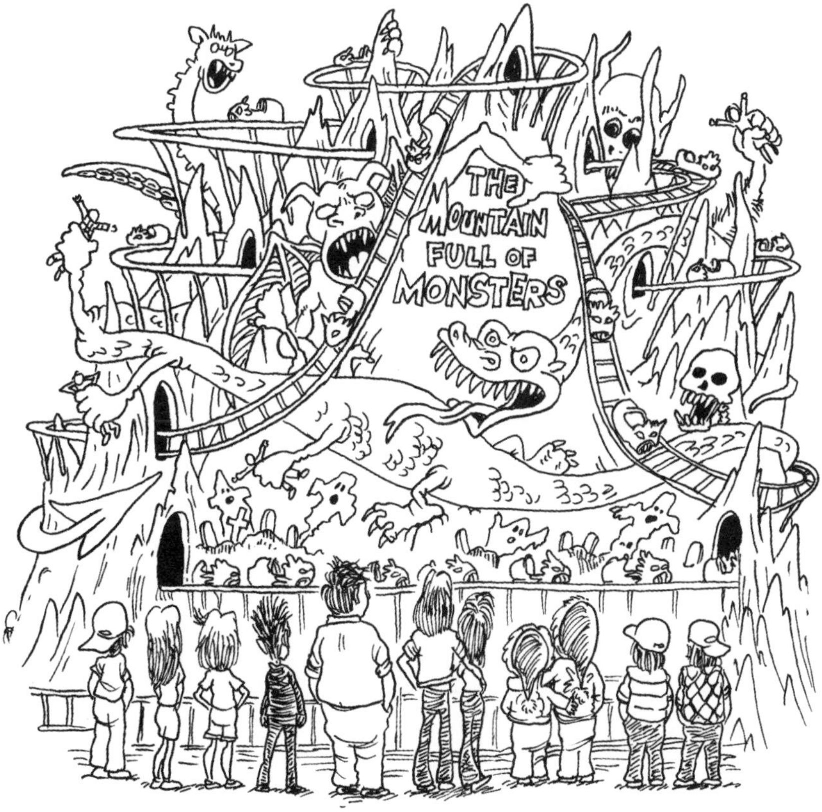
THE MOUNTAIN FULL OF MONSTERS

"Say! How'd all you guys like to take one last spin on her, for old times' sake?" Mr. Humphries says suddenly.

"Just give me a minute to throw the main power switch and get her juiced up . . ." and Mr. Humphries scurries off, still talking to himself.

"Holy crud, dude!" Ricky says to me quietly, grabbing the arms of my shirt. "You're here! Tina's here! The ride's still running! You're getting a second chance!"

". . . you're right, Ricky. It *is* my second chance to get it right."

Well, I still don't know all that much about girls.
But I do know one thing now.
Dreams can change.

30 A NEW BEGINNING

It's over. We've crammed as many monsters as we can fit into the *Santa Express* bus, and we still have some room left for us. They're all ready to start their new life!

Mr. Humphries really is pretty awesome! Not only did he come into the Mountain Full of Monsters with us and point out where to find the best creatures, but he even helped take them out and load them up. Nobody can loosen a rusty screw like Mr. Humphries!

Kyle the bus kid cranks open the squeaky bus door and I jump on board, when I feel a tug at my sleeve.

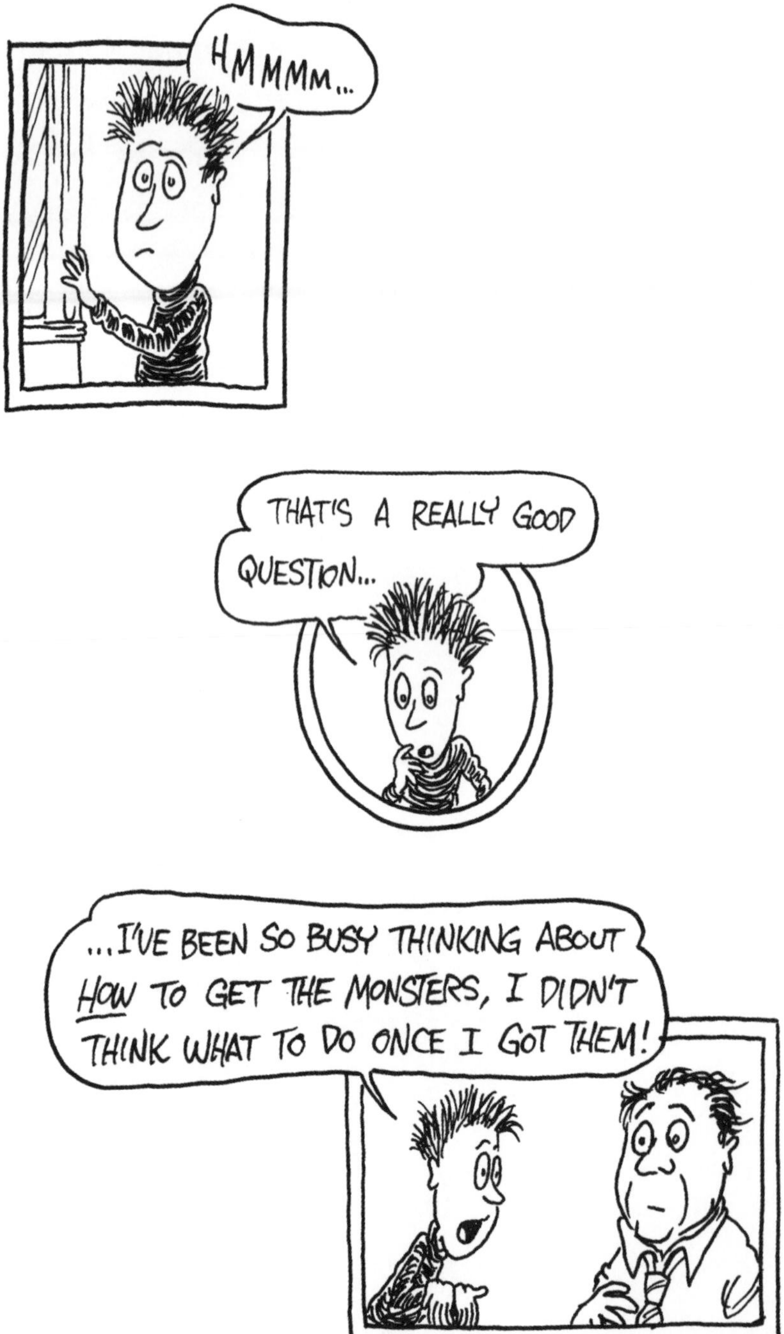
HMMMM...
THAT'S A REALLY GOOD QUESTION...
...I'VE BEEN SO BUSY THINKING ABOUT HOW TO GET THE MONSTERS, I DIDN'T THINK WHAT TO DO ONCE I GOT THEM!

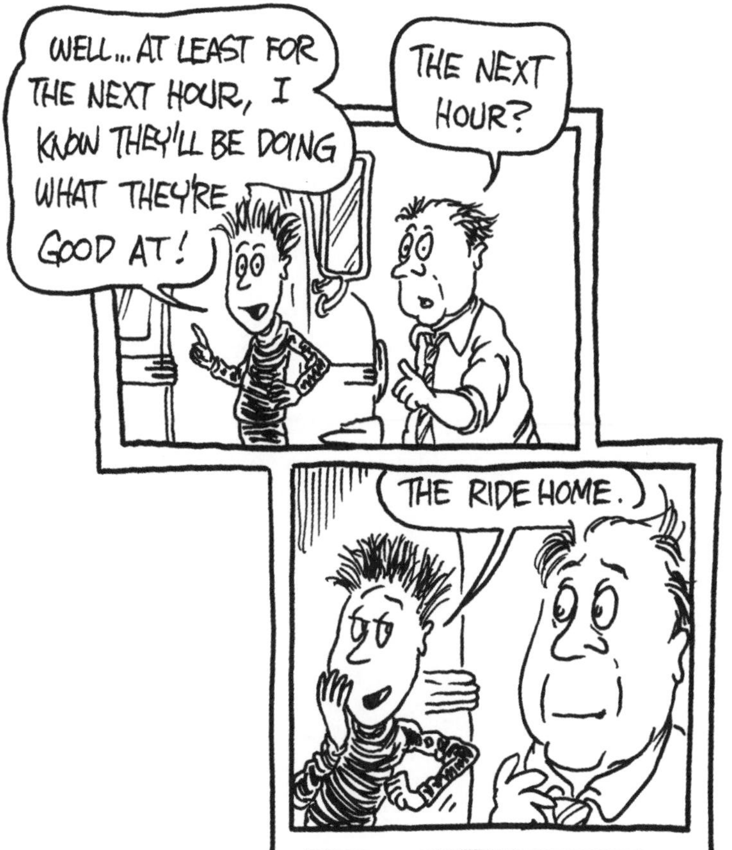
WELL... AT LEAST FOR THE NEXT HOUR, I KNOW THEY'LL BE DOING WHAT THEY'RE GOOD AT!
THE NEXT HOUR?
THE RIDE HOME.

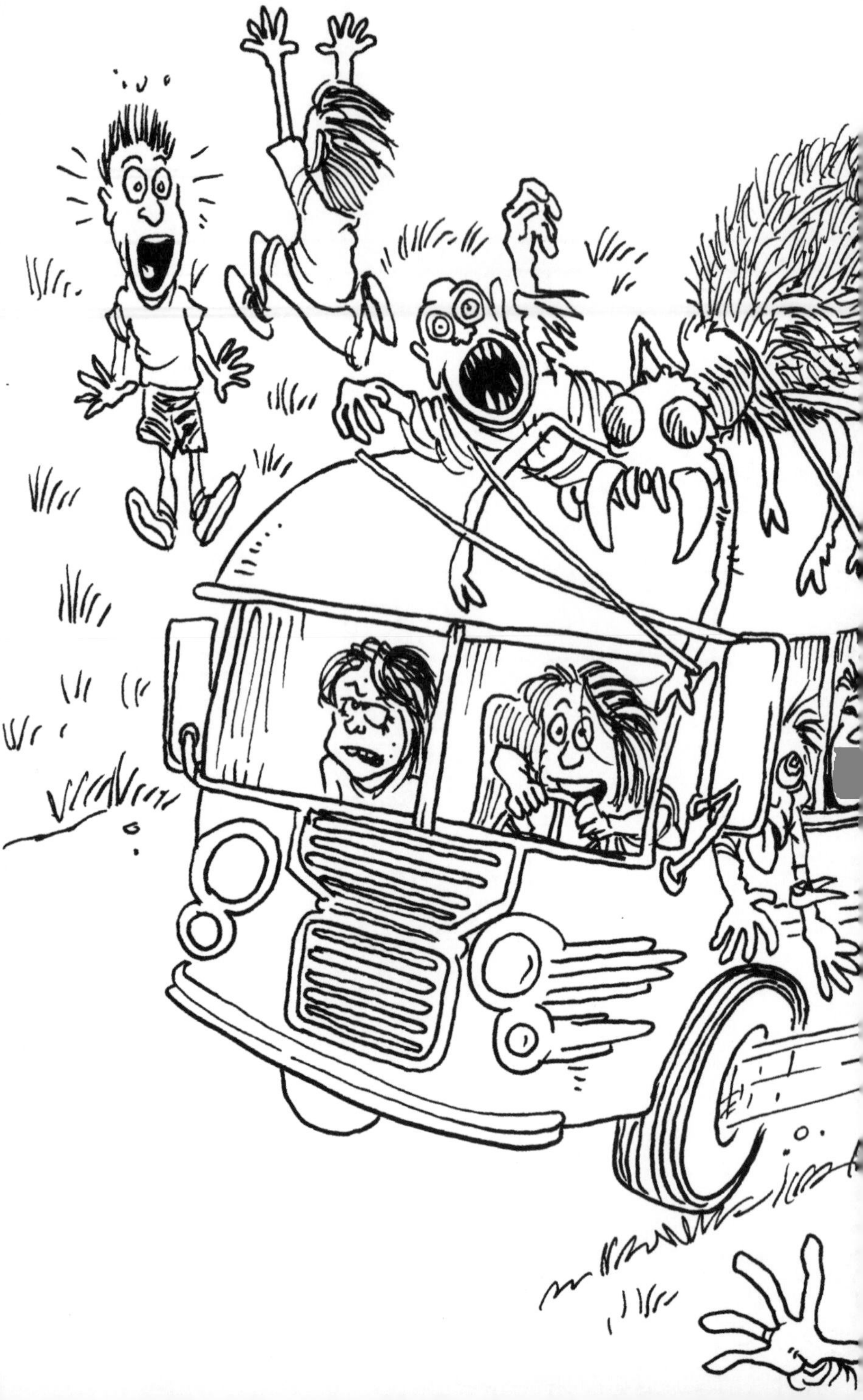

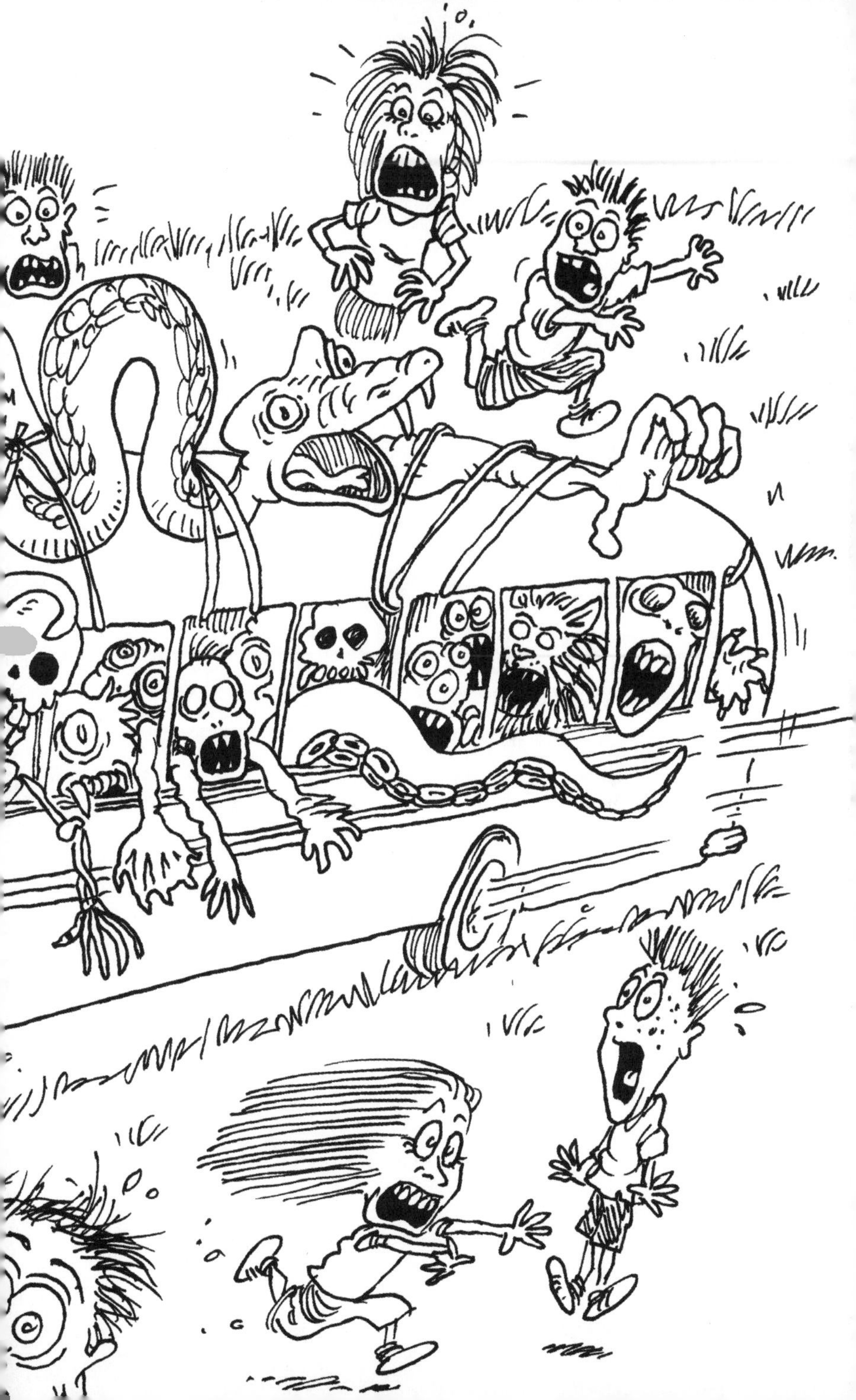

MORE
TO EXPLORE!

MONSTER
Magic, Inc.

MAKE YOUR OWN MONSTER MAGIC WITH DESMOND'S NOTES

I PEED IN THE POOL

SHAZAM!

AAAAAA!

AAAAAA!

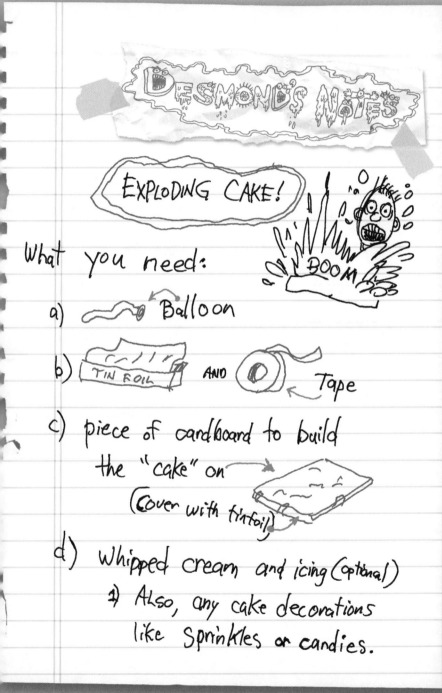

DESMOND'S NOTES

EXPLODING CAKE!

BOOM

What you need:

a) Balloon

b) TIN FOIL AND Tape

c) piece of cardboard to build
the "cake" on
(cover with tinfoil)

d) Whipped cream and icing (optional)
   ⅃) Also, any cake decorations
   like sprinkles or candies.

① First, blow up the balloon

this shape
works best

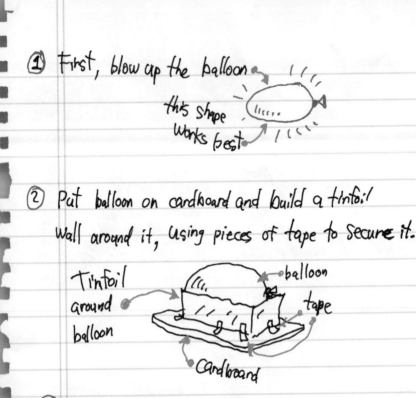

② Put balloon on cardboard and build a tinfoil wall around it, using pieces of tape to secure it.

Tinfoil around balloon

balloon

tape

Cardboard

③ Cover the whole thing with whipped cream (you can mix canned icing with the whipped cream to make it stick easier to the balloon and tinfoil).

ICING + WHIPPED CREAM

lumpy looking cake

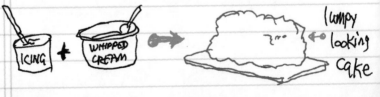

④ decorate cake with sprinkles or whatever you have (it makes it look more _real!_)

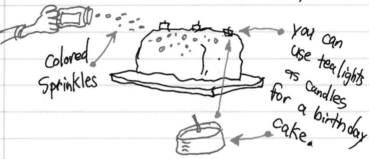

Colored Sprinkles

you can use tea lights as candles for a birthday cake.

⑤ Stand back when somebody cuts the cake!

KA-BAM!

unsuspecting party goer

⑥ Best to do this outside... I don't want your mom getting mad at me, got it?

DESMOND'S NOTES

Spider Catapult!

Here's what you need:

a) wire hanger, the kind you get from the laundry cleaners.

wire all the way around

b) plastic cup and duct tape

c) a handful of plastic spiders (though any plastic or rubber insects will work)

How to make it:

① Bend the hanger down the middle... not
completely in half, just to form a right angle.

Bent
hanger →

← what it looks
like from the
side.

8.

from above

② Bend hook so it holds cup pointing up.
attach cup to hook using tape.

cup

ⓐ

Tape

← hanger

ⓑ

ⓒ (side view)

③ fill cup with
Spiders →

④ holding the the bottom of the hanger flat to the floor, pull cup down

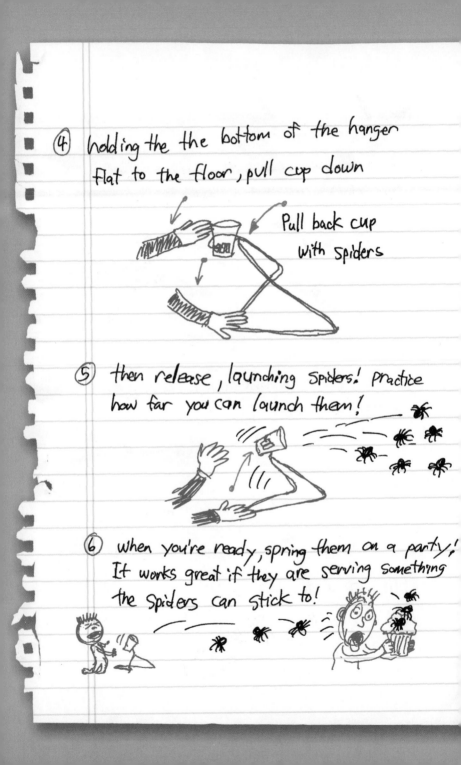

Pull back cup with spiders

⑤ then release, launching spiders! practice how far you can launch them!

⑥ when you're ready, spring them on a party! It works great if they are serving something the spiders can stick to!

LIGHT-UP
ZOMBIE HEAD

✳

✳ this one is sort
of hard, so ask
for help from an
older person if you
need it.

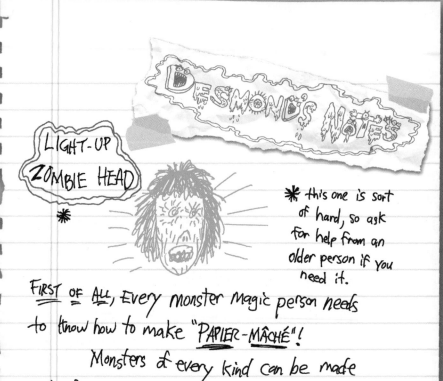

FIRST OF ALL, Every monster Magic person needs
to know how to make "PAPIER-MÂCHÉ"!

Monsters of every kind can be made
out of this stuff, so let's start there:

PAPIER-MÂCHÉ Recipe:

ripped up strips of
newspaper

1 PART FLOUR ✚ 1 PART WATER

MIX

Mix together in a bowl

(I also like to
add some white
glue!)

Now to make the zombie head...
What you need:

Papier-Mâché

newspaper strips

head-shaped balloon

① One at a time, put the newspaper strips in the papier-mâché ⟶

Make sure to wipe off excess.

Papier mâché

② Put the wet strips all over the balloon

Until it's totally covered

③ Make a nose on the balloon by making a small tent shape out of some of the strips.

④ Put the head on a newspaper-covered surface and allow 1 day to dry!

> I need to dry, dude!

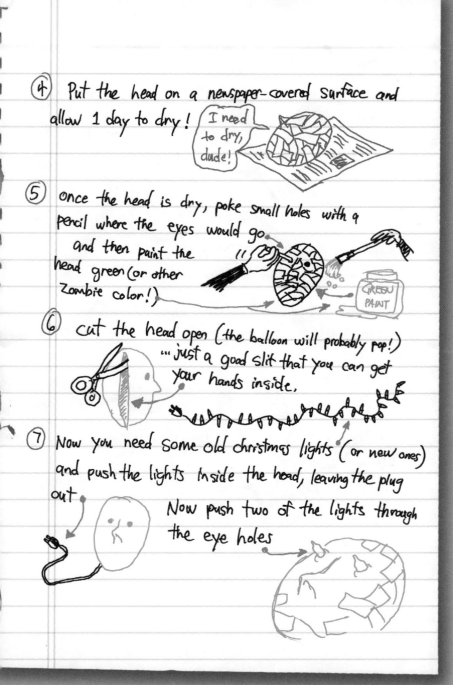

⑤ Once the head is dry, poke small holes with a pencil where the eyes would go. and then paint the head green (or other Zombie color!)

GREEN PAINT

⑥ Cut the head open (the balloon will probably pop!) ... just a good slit that you can get your hands inside.

⑦ Now you need some old Christmas lights (or new ones) and push the lights inside the head, leaving the plug out

Now push two of the lights through the eye holes

8 Now decorate the head with scary teeth and a fright wig (available for cheap at dollar stores or Halloween Shops)

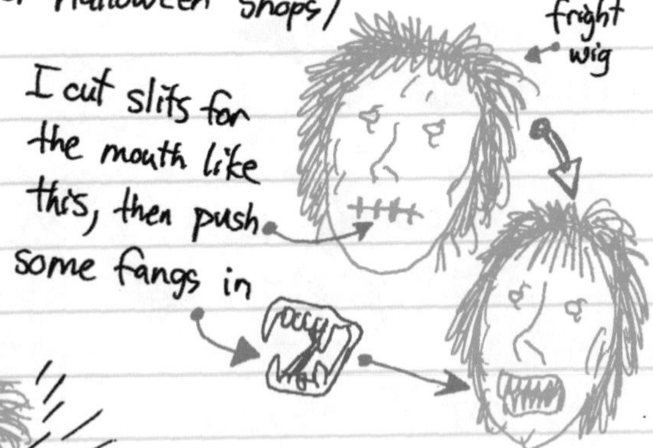
fright wig
I cut slits for the mouth like this, then push some fangs in

9 Now plug it in!
Turn out the lights!
Wait for Screams!

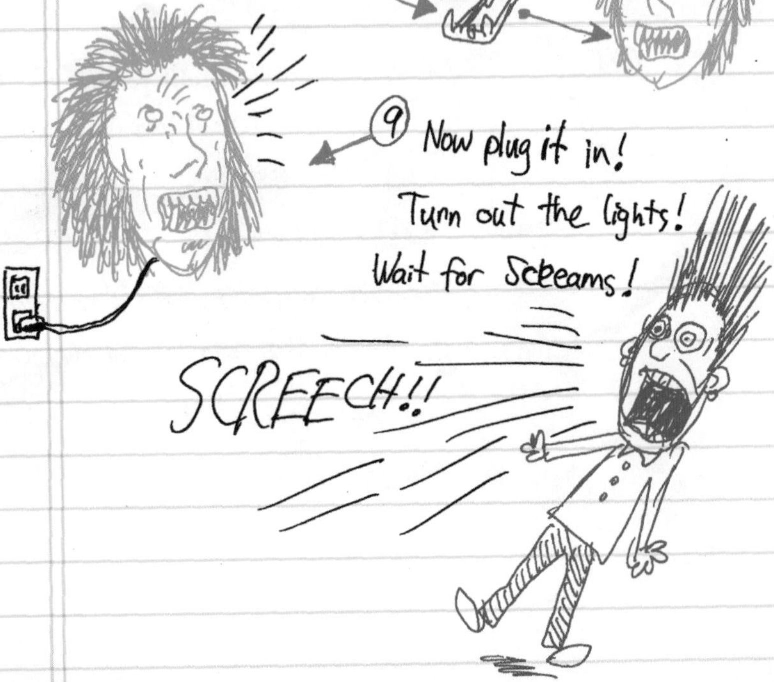
SCREECH!!

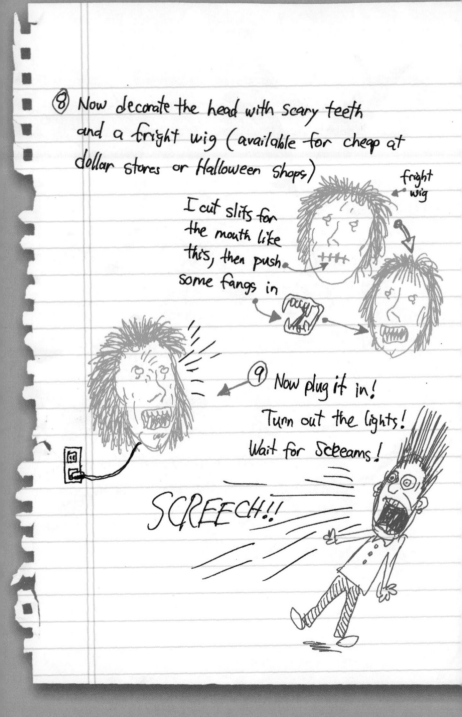

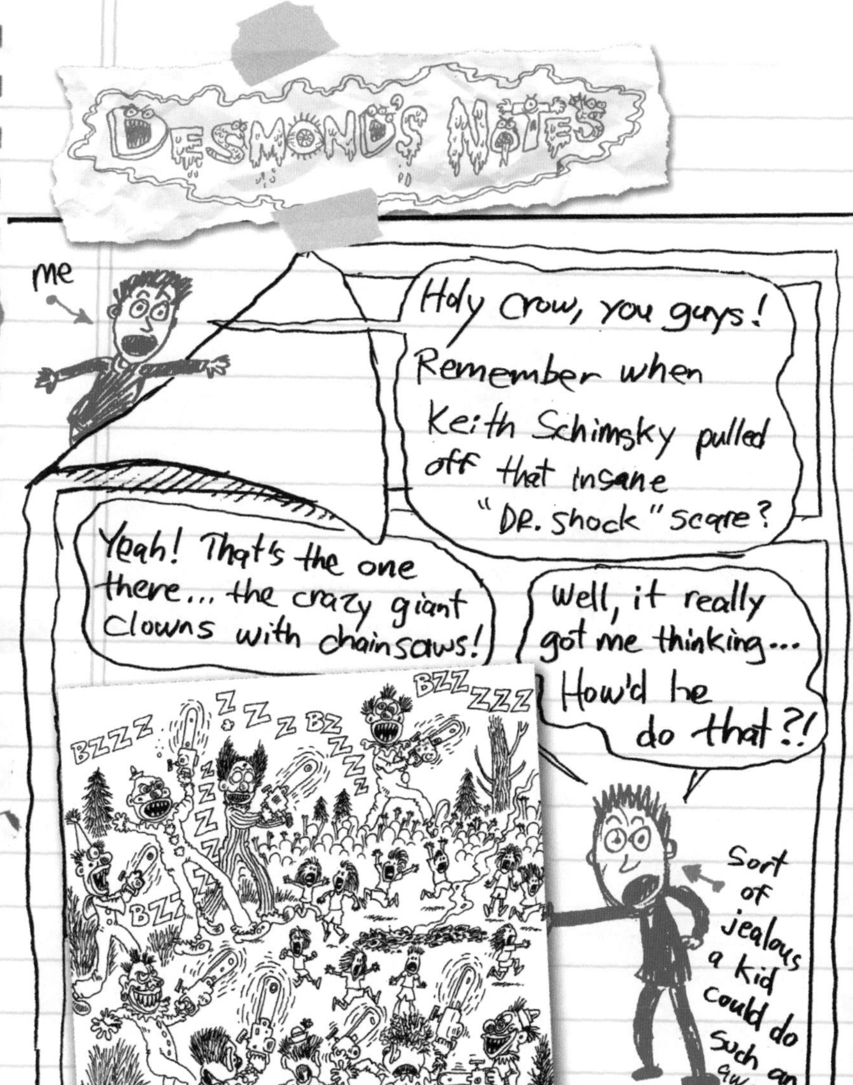
DESMOND'S NOTES
me
Holy crow, you guys! Remember when Keith Schimsky pulled off that insane "DR. Shock" scare?
Yeah! That's the one there... the crazy giant clowns with chainsaws!
Well, it really got me thinking... How'd he do that?!
Sort of jealous a kid could do such an awesome scare
BZZZ
BZZ ZZZ

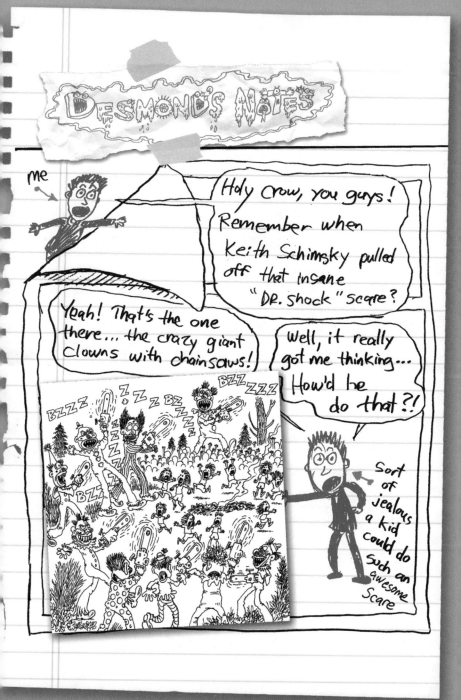

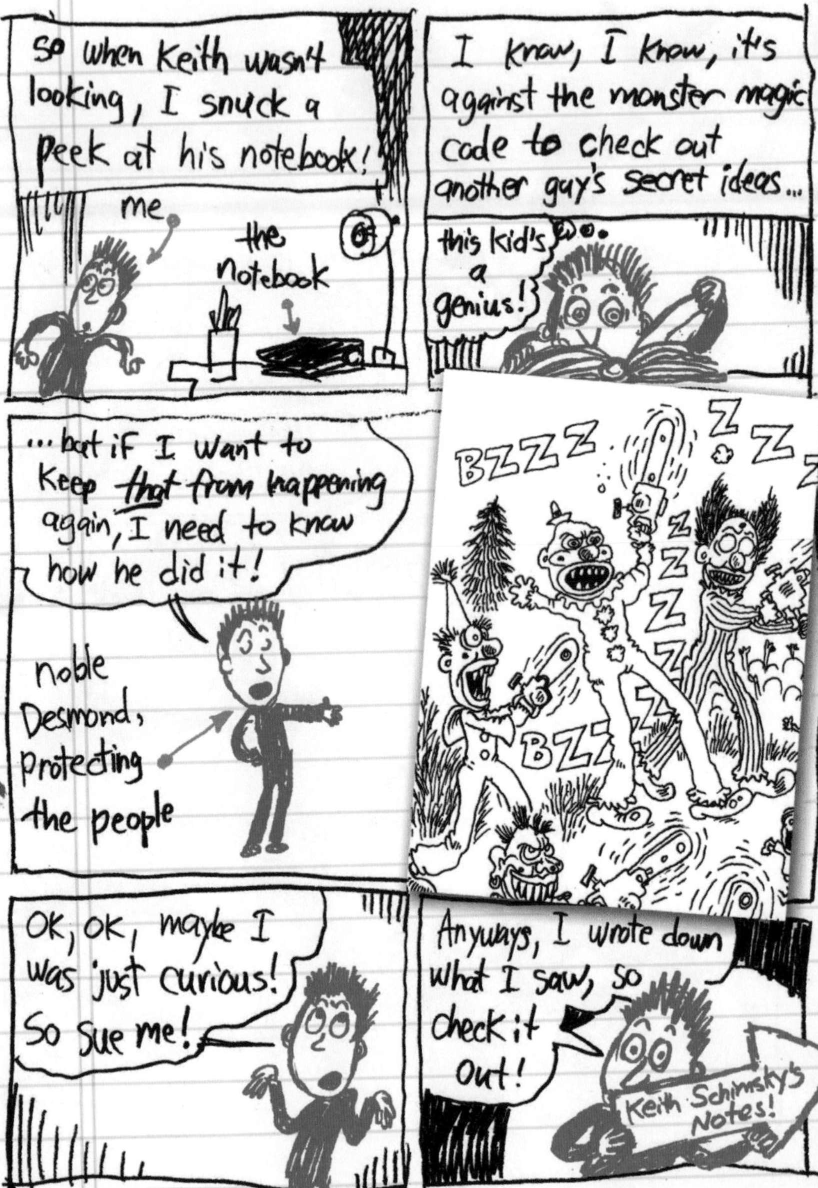

so when Keith wasn't looking, I snuck a peek at his notebook!
me
the notebook
I know, I know, it's against the monster magic code to check out another guy's secret ideas...
this kid's a genius!
BZZZZ
ZZZ
ZZZZZ
BZZ
...but if I want to keep that from happening again, I need to know how he did it!
noble Desmond, protecting the people
OK, ok, maybe I was just curious! So sue me!
Anyways, I wrote down what I saw, so check it out!
Keith Schimsky's Notes!

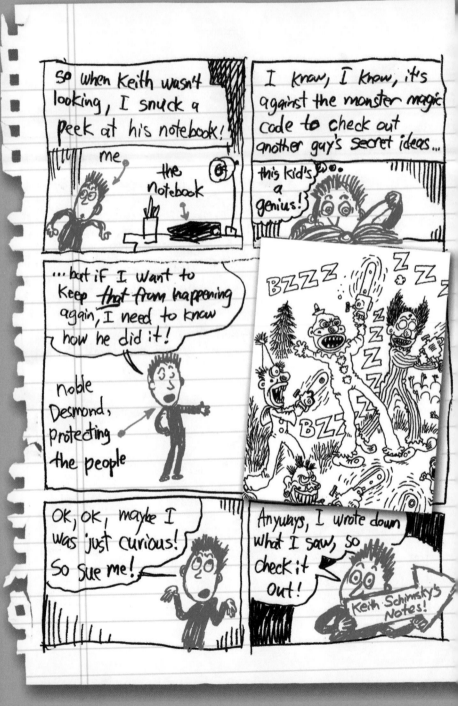

Keith Schimsky's crazy chainsaw clowns

EXPLAINED

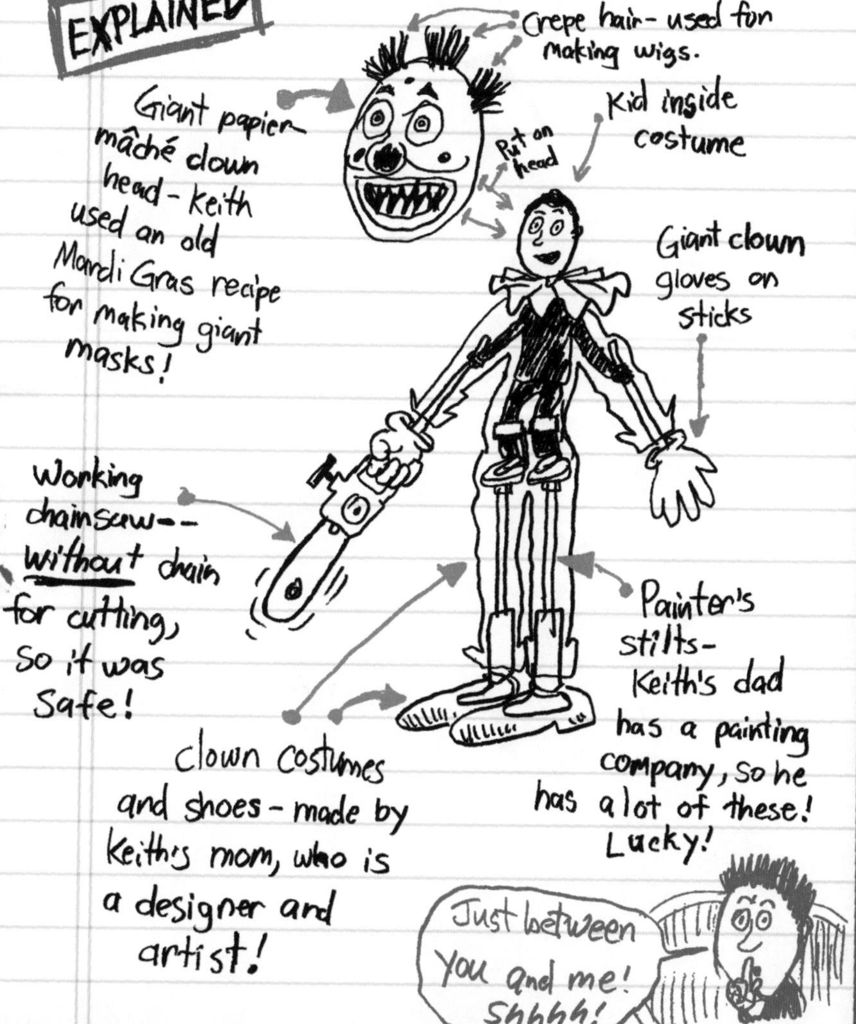

Andrews McMeel Publishing, LLC
an Andrews McMeel Universal company
1130 Walnut Street, Kansas City, Missouri 64106

www.andrewsmcmeel.com

14 15 16 17 18 SDB 10 9 8 7 6 5 4 3 2 1

ISBN: 978-1-4494-3549-3

Library of Congress Control Number:

Made by:
Shenzhen Donnelley Printing Company Ltd.
Address and place of production:
No.47, Wuhe Nan Road, Bantian Ind. Zone,
Shenzhen China, 518129
1st Printing— 5/19/2014

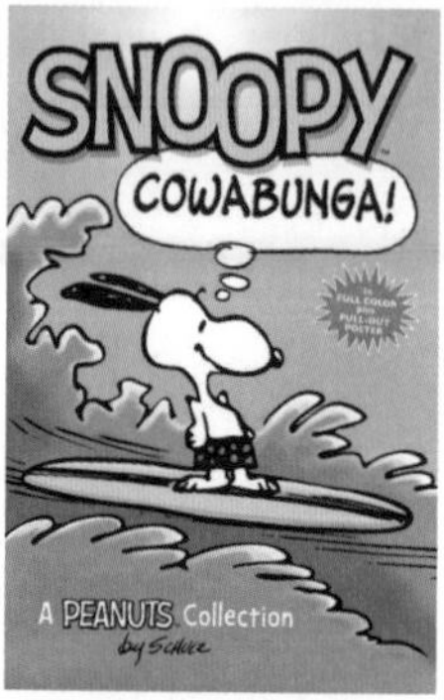
SNOOPY
COWABUNGA!
A PEANUTS Collection
by Schulz

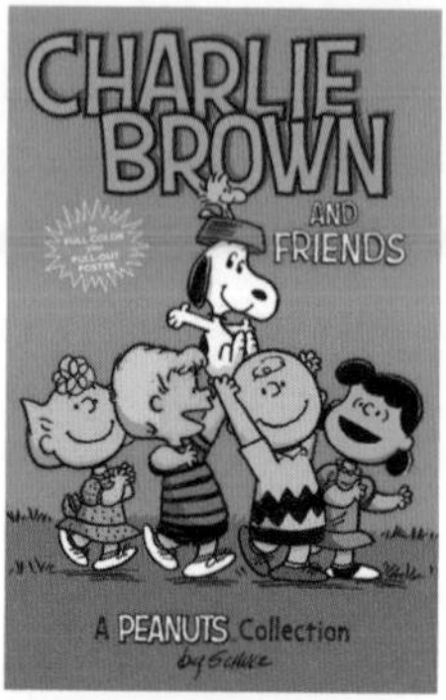
CHARLIE BROWN
AND FRIENDS
A PEANUTS Collection
by Schulz

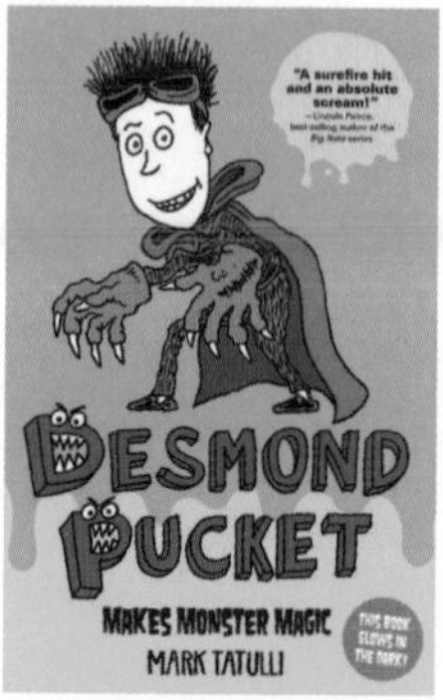
DESMOND PUCKET
MAKES MONSTER MAGIC
MARK TATULLI

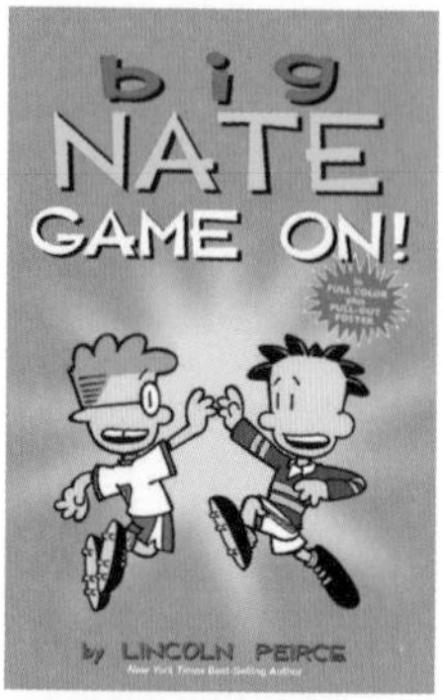
big NATE
GAME ON!
by LINCOLN PEIRCE

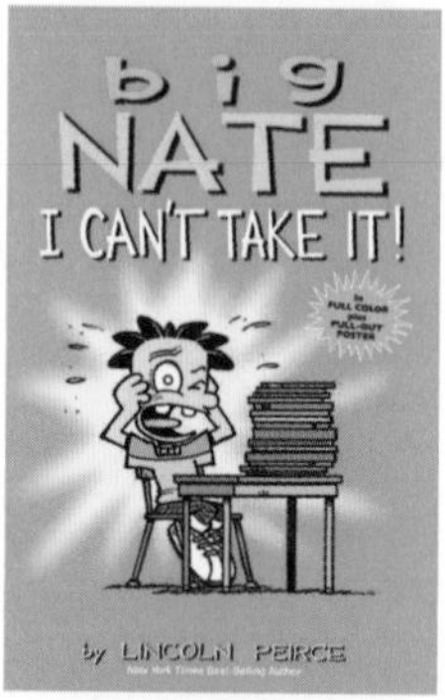
big NATE
I CAN'T TAKE IT!
by LINCOLN PEIRCE

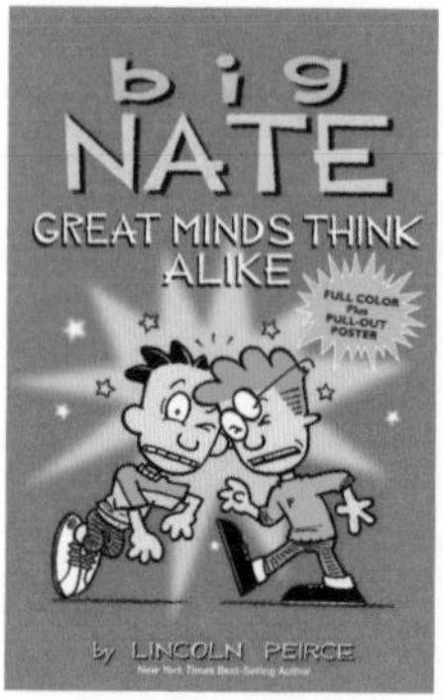
big NATE
GREAT MINDS THINK ALIKE
by LINCOLN PEIRCE

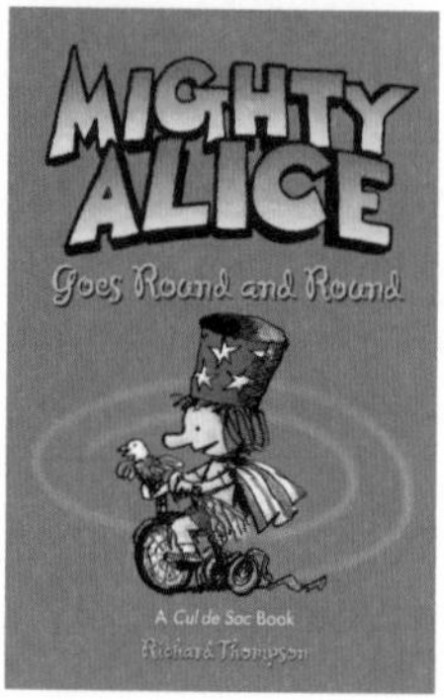
MIGHTY ALICE
Goes Round and Round
A Cul de Sac Book
Richard Thompson

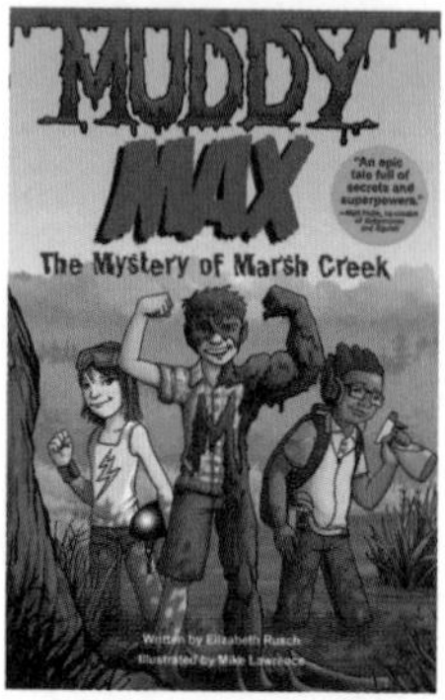
MUDDY MAX
The Mystery of Marsh Creek

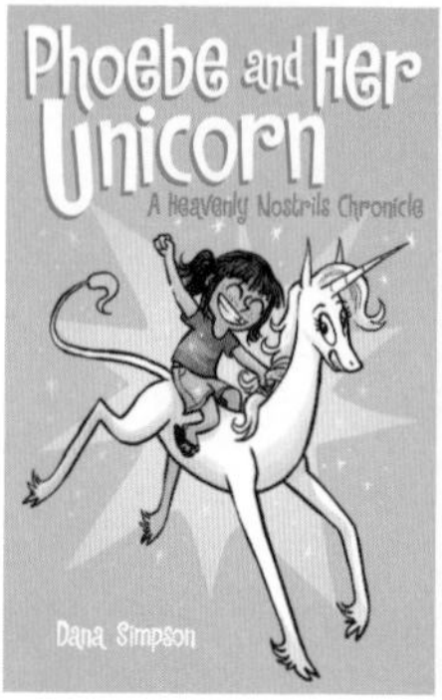
Phoebe and Her Unicorn
A Heavenly Nostrils Chronicle
Dana Simpson

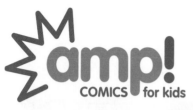

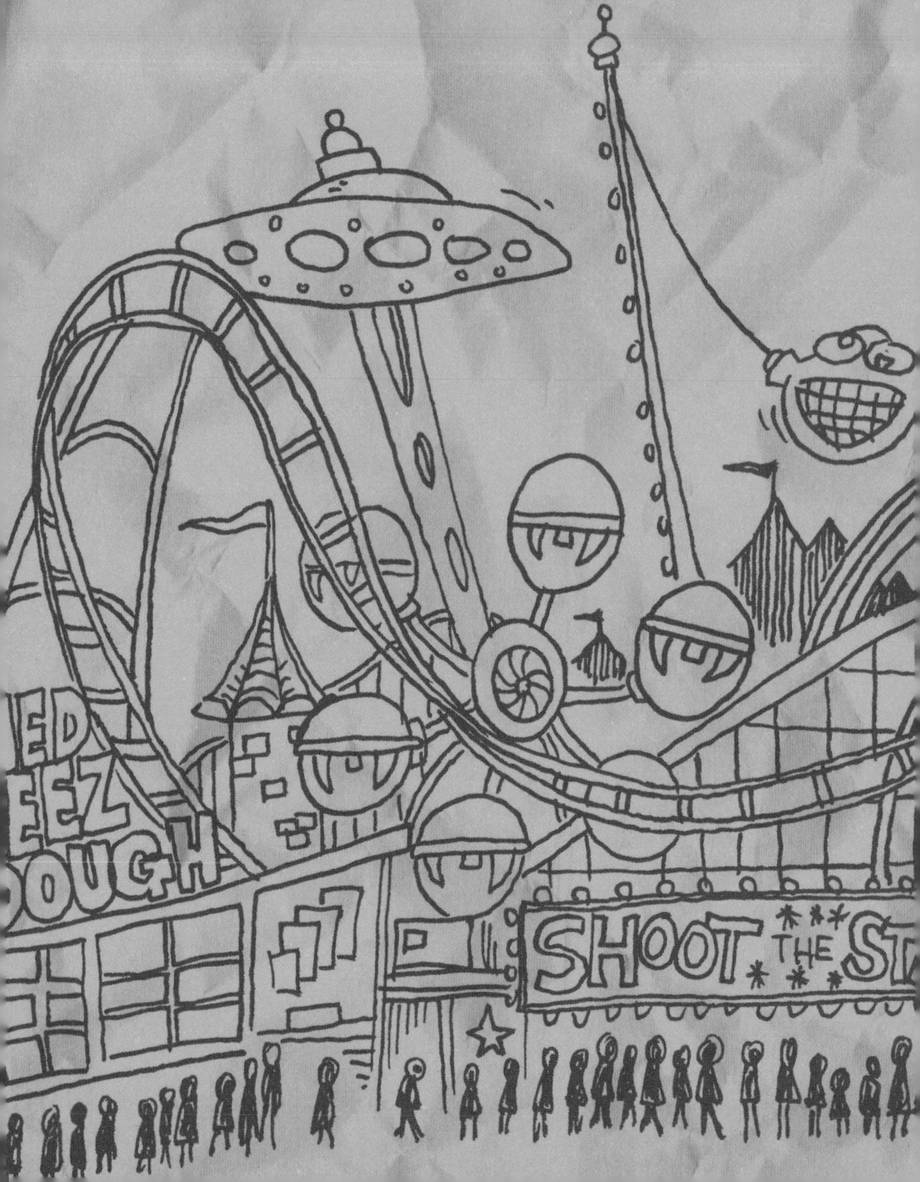
DOUGH
SHOOT THE